THE CHANNEL:
STORIES FROM L.A.

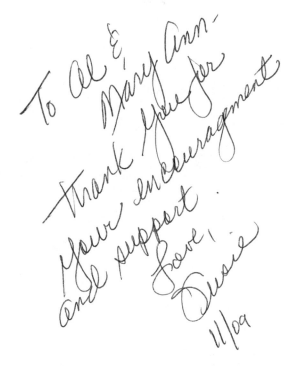

To Al &,
Mary Ann -
Thank you for
your encouragement
and support.
Love,
Susie
11/09

SUSAN ALCOTT JARDINE

Outskirts Press, Inc.
Denver, Colorado

THE CHANNEL: Stories From L.A.
All Rights Reserved.
Copyright © 2009 Susan Alcott Jardine
v4.0

Editor: Donna Pizzi
Cover Design: Blackstone Edge Studios, Portland, Oregon
Creative Director: Donna Pizzi
Digital Artist: Daniel Damocles Wall
Cover Photos: istockphoto.com
"The Monk," Copyright ©, Roberto A. Sanchez
"Blue Space Stars," Copyright ©, Sergii Tsololo
Author Photo: Wilma Camacho Burton

Outskirts Press, Inc.
http://www.outskirtspress.com

ISBN: 978-1-4327-3757-3

Library of Congress Control Number: 2009925511

Outskirts Press and the "OP" logo are trademarks belonging to Outskirts Press, Inc.
PRINTED IN THE UNITED STATES OF AMERICA

CREDITS

AWARDS

"Run for the Money" was awarded Honorable Mention in the Mainstream/Literary Short Story category of the *Writer's Digest* 1999 Annual Writing Competition.

"Hello, You've Reached Amy Byington" was awarded First Place Fiction in the Dorothy Daniels Honorary Writing Award sponsored by the National League of American Pen Women (Simi Valley Branch), 1988.

For my husband, Neal;
my parents, Hazel and Douglas Pearson;
and in memory of my father and stepmother,
William Kenneth and Fern Allin

Contents

Notes

Are we in control of our lives or merely at the mercy of fate? This became the question during the writing of the stories, which were written over a period of several years. Although the stories are works of fiction, this question kept repeating itself over and over as though it were something I needed to address.

It seems that daily we are confronted with myriad losses . . . tiny deaths that slowly chip away at us as the years pass, yet the universal losses are always the same. Global corporations have replaced principalities, and technology gives us a worldview in a matter of seconds. What happens on one side of the planet affects the entire planet. Everything is speeding up, and it appears that we are on a collision course with destiny.

In The Channel collection, Los Angeles becomes the tapestry against which ten stories unravel. It becomes the metaphor and starting place for each of these tales. They take place from the early 1950s to the not-too-distant future. Each of the protagonists experiences life-altering dilemmas. Some are unprepared for their reversals. Others are not. How well they cope is for you to determine. In reading these stories, I hope you can find a little part of yourselves and experience some closure and catharsis.

Susan Alcott Jardine
February 14, 2009

Acknowledgements

These stories were written on yellow legal pads, typewriters, and computers. I wrote them in libraries, coffee shops, on my kitchen table, on park benches, in doctors' waiting rooms, and on my own home office desk. During their writing, I worked for six separate employers, moved out of state and then back again to Southern California, and moved residences about seven times. The journey has been a bit of a bumpy ride.

Without the help and support of the following people, this collection, written over time, would never have been made into this book that you are now holding. It is a miracle, to say the least.

Thank you, Donna Pizzi, editor, writer, teacher, and friend whose editorial eye has touched each of the stories. You have been my Guardian Angel, shepherding this collection through the entire publishing process, including the book cover design. Donna, I am forever grateful. To digital artist Daniel Damocles Wall of Blackstone Edge Studios, you created the most wonderful cover and captured the book's essence. Truly, "A picture is worth one thousand words."

To my dear friend and playwright Marc Havoc, how can I ever thank you enough for your support and encouragement? From our early days, collaborating on screenplays and plays in The Writers

Guild of America, West, Inc.'s Open Door Writing Program; the Playwrights' Unit at The Actor's Studio West; and the late Gardner McKay's Playwright's Unit at The Vanguard Theatre in Los Angeles, we have stuck together through thin and thin. Your spirit permeates these stories. To dear Michael Colton who read early on "The Metamorphosis of Nathaniel Krondstadt" and pointed out the ins and outs of the limousine trade, thank you. To author Harlan Ellison for taking your valuable time to read the galleys of "Metamorphosis" and offer your detailed notes. I am so appreciative.

Thank you to Patricia L. Fry, president of SPAWN, for your book publishing expertise. To the late Marjel DeLauer, literary agent, author, and friend, for your belief and encouragement early on, and to the late Eleanor Sullivan, editor of *Ellery Queen*, "I'm willing to risk the story in EQMM if you are." Thank you to the late Bo Gatewood, the inspiration for the title story. As channel, author, and friend, you shared with me your psychic awakening and believed in my work. Thank you to author Kem Nunn and screenwriter Tom Ricks for your positive critiques so many years ago at The Squaw Valley Community of Writers.

To the late Arthur Alsberg, teacher, writer-producer, and friend, for sharing with our workshop group four of the most exciting and wonderful years of your teaching talent during The Writers Guild of America, West, Inc.'s Open Door Writing Program. I am forever grateful for the experience in the program and for our friendship over the years. To the late Elli Alsberg for your friendship and encouragement and wonderful desserts when we met at your home. You are both a part of this book. To Jeanne Hahn, Dorothy Ghose, and Adria Becker, Artist Co-op 7, for teaching me the art of patience and perseverance. Thank you for your encouragement and support. I wish to thank Deni Sinteral-Scott and the wonderful people at Outskirts Press, Inc., for guiding me through the publishing process. Thank you so much for all of your help. And, a very special thank-you to Howard Junker, editor of *ZYZZYVA the last word: west coast writers & artists* for giving an audience and readership to so many new and emerging voices. You are so appreciated.

A very special thank-you to Margo Stipe, Registrar FLLW Archives, The Frank Lloyd Wright Foundation, Scottsdale, Arizona, for your assistance in my research with respect to the architecture of the late Frank Lloyd Wright. Your valuable time and kindness are very much appreciated.

To the readers of this manuscript during the early drafts, thank you to:

- Don Perry for your hands-on expertise in the music industry.
- Jo Anne Cooper Tuers, partner in crime, at several entertainment jobs. An inspiration.
- Gail and Sharon Bowman for your encouragement and belief in the stories.
- Rowena Buxton-Tauber for sharing the behind the scenes of working for a celebrity.
- Etta weeks for your friendship and editorial comments.
- Anita and the late Lee McLaughlin for your expertise on the entertainment industry.
- My late cousin, Jo Ann Tennant, who pointed out details of the poultry business.
- My cousin Sheila Ramsden for your expertise on the poultry business.

- My late cousin, architect William R. Pauli, for sharing the foundations of architecture.
- Susan Trigg for your first-hand account of spina bifida.
- Stephen Fouce for your expertise on broadcast television.
- Wilma Camacho Burton for your expertise on Community and Public Relations.
- Mary Anne Jennings for remembering Blue Waltz Cologne.
- Tony Tarantino for all of your help.
- Jason Scarcello for reading my work and sharing yours.
- Michelle Allman, Artist Co-op7, for your encouragement and support.

To the members of our short-lived Parkridge Artists & Writers Salon, which had to disband after the Northridge earthquake, thank you for your support and positive critiques:

- Richard Schulenberg, Esq., for your copyright/music industry and writing expertise.
- Mark Weiss for your entertainment, publishing, and writing talents.
- Delaine and Russ Shane for your fiction expertise.
- Beverly Magid for your public relations and fiction talent.
- Tom Culver for your entertainment and book-publishing expertise.
- Caroline Blake for your teaching/artist/curator and writing contributions.
- Dorothy Gordon for your writing talent.
- Mary Goldstein for your artist contributions.

Thank you to Gary Sturm, Iris Mann, Margaret Mary Fitzgerald, Al Jardine, and Pierre O'Rourke, who took time from their busy writing and recording schedules to read the final draft of the manuscript and write the back cover reviews. I am so appreciative.

For my family, how can I ever thank you for bearing with me during the making of this book?

- For my mother, Hazel Pearson, who is the greatest champion of this book.
- For dad, Douglas Pearson, for teaching me how to refinish furniture and for giving us our first real home.
- To Sisala Barbara Williams-Caliguiri for always being there when I was in distress.
- For my wonderful husband, Neal, for giving me our home together, supporting my art, and for being the technical guru on this book.
- To our beloved cats Alex and crew and all of our rescued feral cats, thank you for making life meaningful.

*What could have been a greater profession
than to become an architect? To design
homes in which families could live and
experience their dreams became my calling.
It was the best decision that I ever made
- Billie Marie Kerr, architect. (1940-1998)*

Don't Go Into the Killing Place

I stared out the back window of Henry's Chevrolet coupe and watched Los Angeles slowly disappear. Mama and Henry were in the front seat listening to Frank Sinatra on the car radio. We had just said goodbye to my brother Buddy, who was on his way to Korea a few weeks before. Now I was going to have to say goodbye to Mama too, for the whole summer. I felt so empty with Buddy halfway across the ocean and Mama hanging around her new fiancé all the time.

Buddy had taken me to the beach before he left, and I told him not to go to Korea, that he was supposed to go to architect school, not clear across the ocean somewhere. But he said he'd go to school on the G.I. Bill when he got back home, and then he'd build a house for Mama, Grandma and me. He didn't say anything about Henry.

The sound of Henry's mud flaps slapping back and forth against the coupe's tires made Buddy dissolve from my mind. For a minute, I thought it was Saturday morning and I was listening to the metronome Mama had placed on the high-top piano for me to keep time during my lessons with Mrs. Whitely, and then I realized it was just Jo Stafford's voice mixing with the flap, flap, flap of Henry's mud flaps and not that metronome I could never keep pace with. I stared out the window again transfixed as the city streets melted into row after row of orange groves, saddened by the thought of yet another summer at Aunt Lil's and Uncle Ed's chicken farm. And the sight of those orange groves with their fat, little black soldier sludge pots were not making things any better.

One of the last things Mama had said to me on that hot summer's day was, "Remember, Billie, mind what Ed and Lil have to say, and whatever you do, don't go into the killing place."

I stared her straight in the face. "I won't, Mama." She looked so pretty, her blue eyes shining underneath her new navy blue straw hat, with the white paper rose she had pinned to its brim. Mama was pleased on the day she found that rose at Newberry's Five & Dime. That white paper rose was Mama's new hope for a better life.

She stepped back, smiled, and gave me her secret wink. "It's going to be a great summer for you, Billie; you just wait and see. I promise." She bent down and kissed my cheek.

I can still feel the scrape of her starched white collar brushing against my face and the smell of her Blue Waltz Cologne. The three of us stood there, miles and miles away from home. Mama, me and Henry, who was all spiffed up in his new grey suit, the three of us just standing there on that old gravel road in the middle of nowhere, were searching for something else to say. Mama, hand in hand with Henry, was all fresh and full of hope, dressed up in her special navy blue gabardine suit, with her white paper rose.

I couldn't stop staring at her. She looked the most beautiful I'd ever seen her. A sure-fire double for Ginger Rogers or maybe that new movie star, Marilyn Monroe. Before I could say a word, she and Henry were off in his polished grey Chevrolet coupe, mud flaps whirling in a puff of dust, as I watched them head back onto the highway on their way toward Las Vegas. It was Mama's wedding day, and I'd never felt so alone.

Everybody was gone except for Jessie. My summers at the place were so regular that no one except Jessie was ever there to greet me. Mama thought summers on the farm were good for me. Jessie greeted me with an expectant nod as she looked up from her ironing when I appeared in her sunny kitchen. It may have been Aunt Lil's and Uncle Ed's house, but it was Jessie's kitchen. Her familiar aromas of chicken stew and boiling starch swirled around my head, bringing back the memory of more summers than I could sometimes remember.

"Well, Billie, you know where your room is. Put your grandma's bag in there, then you can come out and help me set the table while you catch me up on the news," Jessie said with her familiar, half-moon smile angled just so it would cover her gold front tooth.

I watched her spindly black arm moving like a water pump handle, pushing the hot iron back and forth across one of Aunt Lil's chintz dresses. It always amazed me how Jessie could juggle ten things at once, ironing, cooking, and keeping an eye out for customers coming up the road to the poultry market, not to mention knowing what you were thinking.

Ever since I could remember, Jessie and her husband, George, had lived in the house back of the place. I think even before I was ever born, Jessie took care of the house and George took care of the chicken farm. She was family to me during my summers there, and I would hang onto our kitchen conversations like a needle and thread sewing pieces of my girlhood together.

I dropped my grandma's imitation needlepoint suitcase onto the yellow linoleum floor and ran my hand down the front of my white cotton blouse to straighten out the wrinkles from the drive.

"Anything popped up there yet?" Jessie teased.

I dropped my hand. "Nothing yet, Jessie. Still as straight as your ironing board."

"Well, wait till next summer. There'll be something there."

"Where is everybody?" I asked.

Jessie just kept pushing the iron back and forth across Aunt Lil's dress. "Well, your Aunt Lil and Cousin Gloria are in town shopping. Uncle Ed is picking himself up some feed at Henderson's Feed & Grange."

I slumped down onto grandma's suitcase and continued to watch Jessie watching me while pretending not to watch me at the same time. "Where's George?"

"In the killing place, I suppose, dressing out some of the capons."

"So you're the only one watching the store?"

Jessie's half-moon smile exploded into a full moon laugh, her gold tooth catching the afternoon sun. "Yeah, Billie. Just you, me, and the chickens."

She finished with the dress and took out a lavender crinoline from the sprinkling bag, spreading it across the ironing board. Her hands moved like a magician's, turning the crinoline across the board while rhythmically slapping the starch brush from the boiling pot across the delicate skirt, turning and slapping, turning and slapping in a drum-like cadence, so as not to burn the fabric. The crinoline sizzled with each touch of the iron and the smell of hot starch wafted into my nostrils.

"Hurry up, girl, take your grandma's bag into your room and get your stuff put away in the cupboard."

I sat steadfast on grandma's case. "How long have you and George been married?"

"Before you were born and then some, girl." Jessie set down the iron. "Don't look so sad, Billie; this is your Mama's wedding day. You should be happy."

"Yeah, I guess so." I rose, picked up grandma's suitcase, and headed toward the back room. I stopped for a minute and turned back toward Jessie, still pushing the iron while stirring the chicken stew on the stove at the same time. "Hey, Jessie!"

She looked up at me with a question on her brow.

"Why didn't Mama invite me to her wedding day?"

Jessie lowered her eyes and continued pumping the iron. "Hurry up, Billie, get your stuff put away. Everyone will be back soon, and we need to get supper on the table."

After supper, I asked cousin Gloria if she wanted to play a game of Chinese Checkers. She primped and fussed with her black curls. "No, Billie, not tonight. I'm going to the movies with Wesley Bingham."

"Wesley Bingham! Gloria, I thought you couldn't stand Wesley. You always said he was a dumb carrot head."

Gloria shook her black curls and squinted her lavender eyes at me. "People change, Billie. He has matured."

"Oh. So what are you going to see at the movies, Gloria?"

"An American in Paris."

"Well, what about tomorrow? How about going over to Mrs.

Heitman's and checking out the barn?"

"Oh, Billie, you're such a kid. Those things are boring. I haven't even been into Mrs. Heitman's barn since you stayed last summer." She held out her right hand and admired her long, red fingernails. "I've changed." She giggled.

"Yeah," I said, forlornly, "I guess you have."

When Gloria had gone the next day, I followed Uncle Ed and George into the holding pen next to the killing place. It was midsummer, dusty and hot. The fuzzy yellow chicks had grown into brilliant, red-feathered hens. They circled to one side of the barbed-wire pen when the three of us entered the gate. Uncle Ed encircled a hen, grabbed her by her feet, and pressed her beak into the dirt. I watched as George took a red-hot cauterizing iron and proceeded to clip the hen's wings. The smell of burned feathers, bones, and flesh pierced my nostrils. The hen squawked and raged, holding her bloodied and burned wings to her side as she ran around the pen in agony. "Why do you have to do that, Uncle Ed?"

Ed and George looked at me like I was a crazy person.

"So they won't fly away," Uncle Ed explained.

"How can they fly away? They're penned up and are just going to end up in the market freezer until someone makes chicken stew out of them. How can they fly away?"

George pulled his red bandanna out from his overall pocket and mopped the sweat that glistened on his crinkled black brow. "That's just it, Billie. These hens do know. They can smell the taste of blood off the ones that went before them. That's why your Uncle Ed and me have to clip their wings, so as they won't fly away. So as they will become someone's chicken stew. It's business, Billie. It's business."

For the next few days, I sort of wandered around and re-explored Gloria's and my old haunts. I guess she was right. It wasn't the same. Even though I traced our adventures from summers past, nothing came together. Everything seemed like it slowed down in a bowl of Jell-O. Try as I may, I couldn't recreate the feeling of those times before. Everything seemed to be changing. I couldn't stop it, so I would help Jessie with the supper and dishes until she was finished with her work and then went home to George, in the back house, and started her work there all over again.

After asking Gloria to join me in Chinese Checkers, Canasta, and other dumb games and being turned down for one reason or another, I decided to just go to my room after suppertime and write.

I looked at the paper with the address my brother Buddy had given me before he was shipped off to Korea. I copied his address onto an envelope.

PFC Budhorn J. Kerr
c/o US Army
P.O. Box 55547
San Francisco, California

June 23, 1952

Dear Buddy,

I'm homesick and I miss you. I don't know exactly how to tell you this, but Mama and Henry went to Las Vegas to get married. It seemed awfully sudden, but I think it will be fine. Henry said he would take care of us now, and Mama quit her waitress job at the Moon Café. Henry said he makes enough at his carpenter's job so Mama won't have to work anymore. She seemed really happy about that.

I would have liked to have gone to their wedding, but I guess I would have just been in the way. It would have been wonderful if they could've waited until you got back home. We could have had a real wedding at a church, with a big party in the back yard. Grandma didn't go either. Her friend Leona is visiting her from Hawaii this summer, and Grandma said they were going to be busy seeing old friends. So here I am at Aunt Lil's and Uncle Ed's chicken farm again.

Everyone here is fine. Gloria sort of sprouted up since last summer. She seems more interested in going to the movies with Wesley Bingham than the stuff we used to do on the place. You remember Wesley, the pastor's son. Aunt Lil says he's from good stock. Jessie said to tell you that she and George say "hi." She said you'll have to tell them all about your travels when you come home.

I just can't stand going into the holding pens anymore. My heart aches to see those innocent little chicks, so trusting when you hold them in your arms, to be fattened up to end up in the killing place. They don't stand a chance. Even though George and Uncle Ed say "It's business," I can't stand to watch it any longer. It just doesn't seem fair, seeing them go off to their deaths summer after summer. It's not like what you're going to do, to build houses for people to live in.

This is going to be an awful summer. I can tell you that. You should be home by next summer. Henry could help build your house for us, I bet. You could talk to him about it when you come home. Since he'll be living with us, we're going to need a bigger place. I wonder if, now that he and Mama are married, we have to change our last name to Peterson. I wonder what Daddy would think of that.

Well, I had better say bye for now. Please write back to me. I'll wait at the box for your letter.

Love,
Your sister Billie Marie Kerr
c/o St. Paul's Fryer Farm
R.R. 435, Lincoln Hwy.
Orange, California

P.S. I've decided never to eat meat again.

"I got a letter from Buddy, today."

"Oh, really," Gloria said. "Why didn't I see it?"

"Because, you lazy girl, you don't get up with the chickens. I waited at the box this morning for the mailman. Buddy knows I'm here, 'cause Mama was going to Las Vegas to get married, and I knew he'd write to me."

Jessie kept cleaning up the dishes and gave me one of her sidelong looks, like she knew I was making the whole thing up.

"Buddy is all the way fighting the war in Korea, and he knows you're here for the summer?" Gloria smirked while pushing her fork at her plate of scrambled eggs.

"That's right, I wrote to him before I came, so he would know where to write back to me."

Aunt Lil finished her coffee and rose from the table. "All right, ladies, we have a full day ahead of us." She straightened the front of her floral chintz dress and picked up her pocketbook from the sideboard. "Come on, Gloria; don't dawdle."

Gloria pushed herself away from the breakfast table and adjusted the waistband on her lavender crinoline. "Well, you'll have to show it to me when we get back, won't you, Billie?"

"Where are you going?"

"Shopping," Gloria replied.

"Shopping? But you went shopping a few days back."

"Gloria is having her coming-out party in two weeks, Billie. We have to find the right dress."

I nodded so as not to look like a total dummy. "Where are you coming out from, Gloria?"

Aunt Lil, Gloria, and Jessie joined in a trio of giggles, alto, mezzo, and soprano. My God, they sounded like the choir at All Saints' Baptist Church!

"What's so funny?"

Aunt Lil patted my hand. "It's a form of expression, Billie dear. Gloria is having her official presentation at The Daughters of the White Rose. She's going to be formally coming out with the other young ladies of the circle."

"White Rose? Are you getting married, Gloria?"

Gloria giggled in her high-tone shriek. "No, Billie, no! I'll explain it when we come back. Then you can show me Buddy's letter."

"Well, we'll see." I sniffed. "It's a very private letter."

"Billie, while Gloria and I are in town, I want you to help Jessie with the housework."

"I thought maybe I could help George, Aunt Lil."

"You're a young lady, Billie. Young ladies don't go into the killing place." With that, Aunt Lil and Gloria waltzed out the kitchen door. Their giggling could be heard all the way to Uncle

Ed's black four-door sedan, until the baboon choir finally died under the grind of the sedan tires screeching along the gravel drive.

I cleared off the table and carried the breakfast plates to the sink. "You know, Jessie, sometimes that spoiled Gloria thinks she knows everything about everything. Well, she doesn't."

Jessie smiled down her half-moon smile and wrapped her spindly arm around my shoulder. "Did Buddy really mail you a letter, Billie?"

"I wasn't lying to Gloria when I said Buddy sent me a letter. I was just wishing, Jessie. 'Cause if you wish hard enough, it will come true."

"Korea is a long way off, Billie."

"I know, but if I wait every morning at the box for the mailman, Buddy's letter will come. It's just a matter of time, Jessie."

I still had the miniature cardboard model Buddy had made during his junior year at George Washington High School. He knew all the way back then that was what he wanted to do-- become an architect and build us our first real home. I kept it in my room. It looked so real. Perfect. Buddy and I talked about it for hours and hours. He even made little pieces of furniture that he carved from balsa wood. "Okay, Billie," he'd say, "you're the decorator." He let me paint the tiny pieces with watercolors and move them around his miniature house. After he was shipped off to Korea, I spent hours in my room moving around those bitty little pieces of watercolor furniture. Grandma had given me scraps from her sewing basket that I made into curtains for Buddy's model home. I wanted to bring it with me to the farm, but Mama wouldn't let me.

For the next two weeks, Aunt Lil's and Cousin Gloria's

search for the perfect coming-out dress turned into absolute pandemonium. "My God, you would have thought Uncle Sam was shipping them off halfway across the ocean instead of to one night at The Daughters of The White Rose Presentation Ball. For the life of me, I couldn't see what was so important.

I never did see much of Uncle Ed during those frantic weeks before the ball. I don't think he could stand the excitement. He seemed to always find a need to go into town for one thing or another. And George was busy supervising the hired hands in the killing place. No one thought I knew what went on out there, but I did. I could hear the chickens squalling when the hired hands cut their throats. I knew what was going on out there all the while. The ladies pretended it wasn't happening. But it was.

All the while, during her coming-out dress frenzy, Gloria totally forgot to ask to see my letter from Buddy, which was just as well, since it had most likely been delayed in the mail. After all, Buddy did say Korea was halfway across the ocean.

I dutifully continued to help Jessie with the housework, between stationing myself at the mailbox, but I was getting itchy to explore other things. One day, while swinging on the rope swing Uncle Ed had hung in the honeysuckle-covered arbor, I couldn't stand it one minute longer. I just began bellowing out and singing "I Love You Truly" at the top of my lungs. The birds joined in like a chorus. It was me and the birds. Me swinging as high as I could, and all of us singing at the top of our lungs. We became a featherbrained choir. I guess we created a really big racket, because some of the hired hands came out from the killing place to see what the commotion was all about. Several of the ladies, wearing blood-spattered rubber aprons, giggled to themselves while I kept on singing and pumping the swing higher and higher. I could smell those sweet honeysuckle vines giving off their warm aroma, covering the awful smells that surrounded the killing place. It was on that particular afternoon Uncle Ed decided I could help him in the brooder room.

For the next several days I was given the task of helping Uncle Ed clean the feed and water troughs in the warm, wooden room that housed the newborn chicks. I loved picking them up and stroking their fuzzy yellow bodies. They were so little and had no idea of what was in store for them. When they were old enough, they would be turned into the holding pen, where they would be fattened up for the kill.

I was just marking time until I could go back home, and was tending to disagree with the fact that Mama felt summers at Aunt Lil's and Uncle Ed's were good for me. Frankly, I was beginning to hate them.

"Hold still, Billie, let me fix the hem." Jessie put a basting tack into the hem of Gloria's lavender crinoline so it wouldn't look like a hand-me-down. Then she adjusted the purple ribbon she had run through the neckline of one of Gloria's white peasant blouses. "There, you look like a perfect dream," Jessie said as she turned me in the direction of Aunt Lil's full-length bedroom mirror.

I gazed at my reflection. Jessie had done wonders, I thought. She made me look good enough for Gloria's coming-out ball. I wished Mama could see me. "Oh, Jessie, I think I look pretty." I reached out and gave her a bear hug. "My outfit is truly beautiful."

Jessie beamed at the results of her transformation. "Now, don't muss up your blouse, Billie." She gently pushed me away at arm's length and shook her head approvingly. "You look as pretty as any of the ladies who will be presented tonight."

The Daughters of the White Rose Presentation Ball was an absolute spectacle of beautiful young women dressed in a splendid array of long white gowns. I thought Gloria was surely the most spectacular of them all. When Uncle Ed escorted her down the ramp to the speaker's stand, she appeared as an angel floating on air. I guess all of her shopping craziness paid off. She was a pure vision draped in layers of white dotted Swiss, voile, and petticoats. She had piled her shiny black hair into a fountain of curls that cascaded down the right side of her head. I swear to God, Gloria looked just like Hedy Lamarr.

Uncle Ed and Aunt Lil glowed while Gloria made her acceptance speech and couldn't stop nudging one another when Wesley Bingham presented Gloria with a bouquet of white roses. Real ones, not paper.

The dance party that followed the young ladies' coming out was a cream puff delight. I watched from the punch bowl sidelines as Gloria and the other girls waltzed in circles around the dance floor. A real band played, and it was a vision right out of a costume movie . . . the dance floor was a sea of white taffeta, silk, and voile--dresses and tuxedos whirling, whirling, whirling and pinpointed by a mirrored diamond ball that spun from the hall ceiling. It certainly was the most spectacular evening of my life.

The next morning my head was still spinning from the night before. I let myself be carried by the arbor swing and felt the sunlight filtering across my face like a mirrored diamond ballroom light. I swear I could hear the music dancing in my head.

"Billieee, Billieee, Billieee!"

I turned in the direction of Jessie's anxious calling as she ran toward me from the house, her apron flying above her dress. "Telephone, Billie, telephone!"

I leaped off the swing, letting it fly behind me. "Is it Buddy? Did he call instead of writing? It is Buddy, isn't it? It is, isn't it, Jessie?"

"No, sugar. It's your mama."

"Okay, Mama, I'll see you in about two hours." I hung up the phone. "Mama, Henry, and Grandma are coming to take me home, Aunt Lil," I said. "I better get my stuff together."

Aunt Lil and Gloria seemed really quiet, not their usual chatty selves.

"Is everything okay, Aunt Lil?"

"Sure, honey. Gloria and I are a bit tired from last night's party; that's all."

"I've got to tell you, Gloria, but you looked just like Hedy Lamarr last night. You were the prettiest young lady at the party."

Gloria stared at the kitchen's yellow linoleum floor. "Thank you, Billie. I'm glad you could be there to see it."

"Gloria, I'll never forget it. It was the most spectacular night of my life. Well, I'd better pack my stuff."

"I'll help you. Billie," Jessie said. "I'm sure going to miss you for the rest of the summer."

"Me too, Jessie."

Aunt Lil, Uncle Ed, Gloria, and I were finishing lunch in the breakfast nook when I heard Henry's Chevrolet coupe coming up the gravel drive. George picked up Grandma's needlepoint suitcase and he, Jessie, Uncle Ed, Aunt Lil, and Gloria walked with me to greet Mama, Henry, and Grandma. Everyone seemed exceedingly quiet for some reason. It felt like a big send-off, not everyone's usual business when I arrived. Henry picked me up and twirled me in a circle, while George put Grandma's suitcase into the trunk of Henry's car.

Mama cleared her throat. "We have some news for you, Billie. I didn't want to tell you over the phone."

"You heard from Buddy. You got a letter from Buddy, didn't you, Mama?" I jumped up and down in excitement.

Grandma began crying, and no one knew what to say.

"It's true. You did get a letter from Buddy, didn't you, Mama?"

Mama pulled me against her breast. "No, Billie, not from Buddy. From . . .Uncle Sam."

I pulled back. "Buddy is okay, isn't he, Mama?"

Mama's hands shook as she fiddled with the latch on her pocketbook. Finally she got it open and pulled out a long white envelope. Her eyes shifted to Henry, who nodded for her to let me see it. "No, honey," she said. "Buddy won't be coming home. We lost him in Korea."

It was as though my ears weren't hearing what she was saying. I stood frozen, clutching the official-looking envelope to my chest. "There must be some mistake, Mama. Buddy's going to write to me any day now."

Mama reached out and put her arms around me. "Billie, Billie--"

"Uncle Sam is going to send Buddy to architect school. Mama, he is. Buddy said he was."

"Oh, Billie, no. No, honey."

"No . . . no . . . no-o-o!" I screamed. *"No, it's not true!"* I broke away and ran toward the killing place. I pushed through the door, startling the hired hands, whose bloodied hands were dunking the newly killed hens into vats of boiling water to soften their feathers. Others were plucking the feathers off chickens on the metal draining tables and cutting off their heads and feet. The bloody hot smells, mixed with chicken gizzards and guts, were suffocating. I pushed past them into the back room. Chickens were dangling, heads down, inside huge tin funnels, blood dripping from their newly cut throats into the catching pans below. I screamed, grabbing two dead hens from their death funnels, and ran past the hired hands out the front door of the killing place.

"I love you truly, truly I do," I bellowed at the top of my lungs, cradling the dead hens in my arms as I pumped the arbor swing higher and higher. The birds joined in, "I love you truly, truly I do." The brilliant, red-feathered hens' blood drained from their stiff dead necks, oozing down the front of my white starched blouse as I pumped the arbor swing higher and higher and higher. "I love you truly . . . truly I do!"

Henry reached out and stopped the swing. I kept singing. He pulled the dead hens away from my arms and handed them to Jessie, who cradled them in her apron. She gave me a really sad look. Tears were streaming down her black cheeks. She kept shaking her head back and forth as she carried the dead hens back into the killing place. Henry picked me up and carried me all the way to his Chevrolet coupe. He didn't seem to mind that my blood-drenched blouse was smearing against his new plaid shirt.

I lay my head on Grandma's soft, everyday lap in the back seat of Henry's Chevrolet coupe and listened to the familiar metronome sounds of his mud flaps tapping away as we drove out of the orange-grove-lined highway toward Los Angeles and home. All the way, Grandma stroked my dishwater blond hair while sweetly humming, "I love you truly, truly I do."

As my body intuitively knew we were approaching 98th Street and home from so many summers away, and with Grandma's soft lap cradling my head, I finally said, "Mama, when I grow up I'm going to go to architect school. I am, Mama. I am."

Mama turned to me from the front seat, next to Henry, and took hold of my hand with hers. "We'll see, Billie. We'll see."

It cannot be denied that outward
accidents conduce much to fortune;
favor, opportunity, death of others,
occasion fitting virtue: but chiefly
the mold of a man's fortune is
in his own hands.
- Francis Bacon. (1561-1626)

The Metamorphosis of
Nathaniel Kronstadt

Nathaniel Kronstadt had just come off a one-month seven-day-a-week bummer. His thirty-year-old skin was stretched taut across his prominent cheekbones. Brittle. Drawn to the breaking point, like the skin of an unoiled drumhead. His endurance had given out two weeks and approximately three thousand miles earlier. Name it, Kronstadt had seen it--twice. He was a Chauffeur for Hire.

His normally perfect leonine amber hair clung to his skull like carrion worms. No one had to ask the man, to know that he was bone tired.

He double-checked the rearview mirror. Seeing it all clear, he whipped a perfect U into the Celeb Limo lot. While easing the Silver Stretch into its allotted space, Nathaniel spotted two other Celeb drivers limping their filthy limos onto the lot. He checked his 14-K Seiko Quartz. It flashed 8:00 A.M., exactly. The end of the line for the three men.

The drivers extended polite nods while going through the ritual of clearing their personal gear from their respective drivers' compartments.

The thought of abandoning Celeb-10 grated deeply inside Nathaniel. He took care of her as if she were his, payment book and all. Although exhausted, he couldn't resist giving her divider window a final shot of Windex and a loving swipe with an ever-ready tissue. Giving her one final appraisal, he then dumped his chauffeur gear into his own baby-blue VW. Ice buckets, plastic champagne glasses, various neatly packaged goodies, and sundries, everything for his clients' comfort--everything within reason. If clients were into heavy stuff, Kronstadt figured they could furnish their own mirrors, razors, and needles. He drove a clean stretch. Whatever they chose to do behind the divider window was their business. As long as their cash was good, their checks didn't bounce, and they didn't throw up on his lamb's wool carpets, it was their business.

Nathaniel jingled the heavy pack of keys against his right palm and dragged his aching narrow body up the stairwell leading to the Celeb office.

He dropped himself into one of the grimy plastic chairs that lined the wall directly across from the dispatcher's cluttered desk. "When is the place going to spring for some decent chairs?" he asked Celeb's owner and morning dispatcher, Harry Goldfind.

Without looking up from his bank of phones, Harry shifted behind the laminated walnut desk. He finished dispatching four pickups to four drivers in the field while keeping two clients happily waiting between hold buttons. Harry was a master of the trade. He believed in "the long dollar."

Nathaniel simply watched, a big bush cat surveying his quarry. He loved the game Harry played with him. He allowed long silences between the boss and himself. He knew it unnerved the old man. Like the great cats, Nathaniel Kronstadt rested until it was time to spring.

"The new Fleetwoods are on the showroom floor, Nate. You wanna go see?" Harry finally squeaked his chair in the direction of his number-one driver.

Nathaniel closed his eyes and sighed. "Colors?"

"Yeah, colors. Golds. Burnished greens. Earth colors, just like you suggested." Harry panted. Sweat sprang from his creased brow. He flicked it off with a fat forefinger. "Pinstripes, too. What do you say, Nate?"

Nathaniel's face registered nothing. Harry was the only person allowed to call him Nate. To everyone else, it was Nathaniel.

"Soon."

Their game was interrupted by the phone. Harry took the rush order with charm and diplomacy. He was the best. He quickly dispatched the order to a free man in the field.

"Smitty, get ready to copy. I don't care if you made your last drop. This is important. Pick up Mr. Fazi Talla at LAX in an hour, on British." He rolled his eyes. "I don't know what he looks like! What does a sheik look like? Hold up a damn sign! Come on, Smitty, show some class. The bell captain at the Beverly Wood asked for you. You got a week's possibility. They want transport to the Springs."

Harry clicked off the mike and shook his head in exasperation. "Rookies. They drive you nuts."

Nathaniel made a mental note of the sheik's name. A small uncertainty jabbed at him. Why was Smitty requested? Why not him? He smiled at Harry.

"How soon, Nate?" Harry pressed. He'd always relied on Nathaniel's taste in Fleetwoods.

"As soon as I steam the world off my bones and get ten hours' sleep."

"You know, your insane schedule is gonna land you in a sickbed."

"You worry about it here; I'll worry about it out there. I know my limits."

Harry curled his lower lip. "You'd better. You're the only man I have who insists on working through off-time. It's gonna kill you. Too much greed, Nate."

Nathaniel stretched his spine. "Yeah? It depends on what side of the wheel you're looking from, Harry. Everything is relative."

Nathaniel stood and stared down through the streaked window. Celeb-10 waited below. An aching came over him and lodged in his chest. He always felt an overwhelming sense of loss when he had to abandon her to another driver. She was his baby. He cringed at the idea of someone else exerting power over her pure, silver body. She carried him past all boundaries of time. Behind her wheel, Nathaniel knew he would never die. He had worked it out numerically. Celeb-10 translated into one. As long as he was within her confines, he would live forever.

It had begun eons ago. A spark ignited and a soul came into being. Translucent, silica crystals that had once been stone shone beneath Nathaniel Kronstadt's narrow body. He gave himself up as a sacrifice to blazoned yellow skies. He balanced atop a sacrificial altar of an ancient Aztec pyramid, pure, untouched, clean for all time, and a driving energy reigned silently within him. It had been written into his code before he had come into being. Reality would be Nathaniel Kronstadt's enemy. He listened to the methodical rhythm of his own heartbeat. White silence enveloped him. He waited patiently for release. The rising odor of musk piqued his nostrils.

He had parked his blue VW near the entrance to the Beverly Wood Hotel. He snapped the aluminum tanner shut. The heat had activated his aftershave cologne. Musk, mixed with his tired body toxins, overwhelmed his frail, exhausted frame. It overpowered him. He glanced at the cabs lined along the curb and then checked the magnetic deli sign he had clicked to the outside door of the VW. It was still in place. Dan's Deli, 24-Hour Deliveries. He smiled. None of the cabbies would wedge him out. They would assume he was there to make a delivery. He checked his rearview to see if the tanner had put some color back into his taut face. It had.

Allowing for traffic and waiting for luggage at LAX, the number in the sheik's entourage, and the tie-ups on the 405, Nathaniel figured that Smitty should be pulling into the drive within the next few minutes. Nathaniel was precise to a fault. His timing was near perfection.

As he brushed his hair with his genuine boar-bristle brush from Fred Segal's, he caught sight of Celeb-2 pulling into the curving drive. He flipped his brush into his Gucci travel case, pulled the deli sign inside the VW, and watched.

Sheik Fazi Talla, flanked by four sphinx-like men of various shapes and ages, paraded before Nathaniel's rearview and disappeared into the gaping mouth of the coral albatross. Nathaniel strained to pick up a thread of their conversation, but to no avail. Their fading cacophony was foreign, ancient. Sounds dead to his ears.

He watched as Smitty and two bellmen trudged behind, groaning against the endless weight of designer luggage, like desert beasts of burden. This was one of the many embarrassments Nathaniel despised about his trade. He longed for elegance.

Without warning, a blood-red fingernail jabbed at the crease in his jacket. Carla tapped icily at his shoulder.

"Hi, sweetie. What brings you to my favorite watering hole, as if I didn't know?" She laughed huskily.

He hated Carla's laugh. It cut through him like a harrowing wind. He gave her a disapproving look and prepared himself for the hustle.

"Honey, you can't hide that little calculator in your head. It shows in your eyes. Sweet little Nathaniel, always casing a potential mark."

Nathaniel stared straight ahead without looking at her. She glared at him and flipped her streaked mane of hair. "My afternoon sugar should be pulling up any second."

He hated her, but between them it was strictly business. Carla hadn't stiffed him--yet. An arranged love match was always good for a quick $60.00.

Sugar drove up right on cue. Nathaniel recognized the plates on the 450-SL. It was a rental. Sugar was a real sport.

"Don't forget what I said, Nathaniel honey. I caught you eyeing the posh parade your rookie hauled in."

Nathaniel cringed. "I'll check it out, Carla," he snapped.

She smiled. "Just leave word with the barkeep at C&C's and there'll be a little something extra in your Christmas stocking." She blew him a kiss and shimmied her expensively wrapped body into the waiting 450-SL.

Smitty registered surprise when he saw Nathaniel lounging

against his limo. The young driver loosened his tie and removed his rumpled jacket. Nathaniel appraised his attire. "Simple man," he thought to himself.

"Hey, Nathaniel. You're the talk of the grapevine. The guys are laying bets you won't be able to keep up the pace."

"I gotta keep my baby in diamonds," Nathaniel quipped.

Smitty grinned. "What woman would put up with your crazy hours?"

"I have bigger plans. No station wagon full of bawling kids for me." He'd hit Smitty's wing. He gave him time to ponder his trapped existence.

Smitty pulled at his tie and lowered his eyes. The smile left his voice. "Yeah. It's hard going home after seeing this day after day."

"How would you like to cut in some extra tips?"

Smitty's eyes widened. "How?"

"Would the sheik like to fall in love?"

Smitty was slow on picking up the gist. A three-month rookie. Nathaniel grew impatient. He handed Smitty a slip of paper. "Here's my number. If your man wants to fall in love, give me a call. There's a machine on it. If he does, there'll be a little something extra for your kid's Christmas stocking."

He didn't wait for Smitty's answer. He had planted the seed. It would just be a matter of time before Smitty called.

Nathaniel drove east on Sunset. He wished his VW had cruise control like Celeb-10, because then he could program his homing device, lean back, and let himself be carried. He ached for the Silver Stretch. Inside her, he was safe from pain, safe from rejection, safe from the world. He trusted her completely. He knew her every sound. He knew what Celeb-10 needed before any of the dials registered their lack on her sleek ebony dash. She kept him safe from the unconscious terror that grabbed his throat while he slept. As long as he was protected in her silver womb, he knew he wouldn't die.

A traffic tie-up snapped him back to the reality of the Strip. After a weary ten minutes of it, he made the left turn into the parking area beneath the Serene View Apartments. While Nathaniel parked, he spotted the new tenant getting into her lime-green Impala. Her permed hair overwhelmed her small, tanned features. Nathaniel eyed her with curiosity. His normally precise manner gave way to the most erotic of fantasies. He nodded politely as she slid into the driver's seat. She felt his penetrating stare burn into her left temple. She returned a neighborly nod before driving the Impala out onto the street.

An aspiring starlet, he thought to himself. He hadn't missed the beat-up suede portfolio she had tossed onto the back seat. He couldn't understand why the young woman didn't take the time, money, and effort to invest in an expensive portfolio. After all, it carried her dreams. He thought she looked like perfection driving off--and brushed the thought away. Her portfolio gave her away. He always looked for flaws. It gave him the excuse to avoid intimacy at all costs.

Aside from Celeb-10, Nathaniel Kronstadt's universe consisted of a 25-inch Sony Trinitron with an accompanying VCR. Its Stop-Action-Replay button allowed him total control over his electronic world. Without thought, he flipped on the TV the instant he entered his dim apartment.

A commercial oozed across the screen and snapped into focus. It was the new tenant, seductively mouthing copy for some hair spray. A handsome actor moved into the shot and caressed her raven hair. Nathaniel was overwhelmed by a surge of jealousy. He furiously pressed the sound switch to hear what they were saying. He felt betrayed. It was too late. She and the actor dissolved into an afternoon soap. Betrayal was replaced by cunning. He berated himself for not being quick enough to tape it. He was entranced by her. She was on TV. A bronze goddess seducing him in his 25-inch color world.

As he slid into a steaming tub five minutes later, his mind was still on the new tenant. He began to prepare the script. It must appear spontaneous. He would wait by the pool until she returned. He would tell her how wonderful her commercial was and offer to tape it on his VCR. Of course, she would be flattered. The scenario played beautifully. They would date, fall in love. It was perfect, in his head.

Smitty paced outside the Koshinara Restaurant atop the Beverly Center promenade. Sheik Fazi Talla's secretary had asked to meet him there for lunch. Soon the impeccable pinstriped man arrived, carrying an attaché case. Smitty remembered the petite man from the sheik's entourage. He spoke perfect English.

Smitty fussed at his mail-order vest as Atalla gracefully swept up portions of the picturesque cuisine with his chopsticks. Smitty was out of his league and prayed that it didn't show. He needed this job. He was two months behind in the rent, and Marie was pregnant again.

Atalla had his mark. "You see, my dear Mr. Smith, Sheik Fazi Talla is a very powerful man in our country, yet he has, how shall I say, a great feeling of patriotism for our land. It saddens him to know of the civil strife that his people are encountering." He paused and directed his deep brown stare into Smitty's pale-blue eyes.

Smitty attempted a weak smile, gave up fumbling with his chopsticks, and reached for a fork.

"Although our short trip to Palm Springs is for land, metaphorically speaking -- our business meeting has long-term effects."

Smitty was absolutely confused, yet he played at listening intently as though big business deals were an everyday part of his life.

"I hope you've chosen an associate of a discreet nature?" Atalla ventured.

Smitty choked on his rice. "Oh, yes! He's the top driver in the company. Very polished, sir."

Atalla sipped his tea and touched the linen napkin to the corner of his lips. He smiled. "Good."

Nathaniel turned on the faucet and let scalding water pour into the cooling bath. Every tired muscle, sinew, and bone was beginning to relax. He drifted.

"The water is burning me, Auntie! Please turn it off!" the child shrieked, his skin turning red in the scalding, claw-footed tub. Aunt Ruth bent her voluminous body over her scrawny six-year-old foster son. She scrubbed him unmercifully. Nathaniel squelched the cries deep inside his throat. He knew the ritual.

"Keep away from those Hortense girls," she bellowed. "They're filth! Scum of the earth! Look at their mama--men coming and going at all hours!"

"We were just playing jacks, Auntie--that's not bad," he pleaded.

She shook his frail shoulders. "Filth! If you go near that house again, I'll whip you so you'll never sit down again!"

Nathaniel shut off the hot water and poured some gardenia

crystals into the bath. Suddenly the familiar chill pierced him. He felt weak and cold in the steaming water. He knew the new tenant wouldn't be any different from all the others.

Human contact had become a marathon of disappointments for Nathaniel. Unconsciously he programmed intimacy to end in betrayal. This pattern was tripping up his precisely planned world.

The phone rang. It was Smitty.

"I've decided to go for your idea," he said.

Nathaniel smiled to himself. "When?"

"The sheik needs two limos for a trip to the Springs. A land deal. I'll tell Harry they requested you. Meet me at the Beverly Wood with the love match Saturday at nine A.M. Sharp.!"

"You're a smart man, Smitty. I'll see you." Nathaniel hung up the phone and set his digital alarm to ring in ten hours.

A vision of the new tenant floated across his mind. She smiled at him from the passenger seat of Celeb-10. He returned her smile and drove deep into the desert. Celeb-10 shone brilliantly in the sun. Suddenly he felt sick. "Don't!" Auntie Ruth's voice reverberated in his ears.

It was 9:30 A.M. The two Celeb limos, with their expensive cargo, careened down Highway 10 toward Palm Springs. Nathaniel's usual confidence wavered. He set the Silver Stretch on cruise control and strained to hear the conversation that faintly trickled through the imperceptibly cracked divider window.

The sheik, a bodyguard, Atalla, and Carla were unaware that the divider window was slightly ajar. Carla's syrupy voice melted across the men's halting, thickly accented English. Nathaniel caught bits and pieces. "Drop . . . meeting place . . . " It was hard to make out, but he soon realized that it wasn't a land deal.

Nathaniel's eyes darted between the road, Smitty's limo cruising ahead, and the rearview mirror. He stifled a gasp when Atalla's attaché case flipped open, revealing stacks of crisp bills. He remembered Harry's words, "Too much greed, Nate."

Before he could formulate a plan, the familiar Hadley Orchards sign loomed ahead and Smitty's limo signaled a left turn onto a side road just past the landmark. Nathaniel released the cruise control and followed Smitty's lead, wondering where the rookie was taking them.

A helicopter and two men were waiting about ten miles down the isolated road. The late-morning sun burned white. Nathaniel flashed on Apocalypse Now. The helicopter looked like a giant locust waiting to swallow them in the wasteland. A shiver ran through his bones. He pulled Celeb-10 up behind Smitty's parked limo. He was scared. Something heavy was going down. Quickly, covering his nervousness, he stood dutifully at the passengers' door as the sheik and his two men slid out and moved forward to greet the others waiting by the helicopter.

Carla came up beside him, laughed, and touched up her makeup. "What's the matter, sweetie? Cat got your tongue?"

He ignored her and pulled Smitty aside. "What's going on?"

"Keep it down," Smitty insisted.

"This is no land deal." Nathaniel didn't lower his voice.

"Don't blow it," Smitty warned, taking Nathaniel's arm and turning him so that his back was to the others.

"I want to know what's going on," Nathaniel demanded, "rookie."

Smitty laughed, and without warning Nathaniel felt a metallic thud at the back of his skull.

With the impact came a rising smell of musk. Suddenly

Nathaniel felt pure, free from weight. He called out, but no one paid attention. He watched them dump his limp body into the trunk of Celeb-10.

The sheik took off in the helicopter with the two men. Carla and the others waited in Smitty's limo while he meticulously wiped their traces clean from Celeb-10 and then radioed in.

"Harry," he said. "I just dropped at the Springs. The sheik changed his mind. I'm heading back. Incidentally, Kronstadt never showed at the Beverly Wood this morning. I know he's your top driver, Harry, but the guy let us down. I think he's been overdoing."

Smitty scattered their footprints with a piece of bramble before driving back to the main highway.

Nathaniel Kronstadt screamed out to Harry Goldfind. "I'm here, Harry! I'm here!"

There wasn't a sound. Nothing. Only white stillness followed by a whir of circling sand. And then again nothing.

Nathaniel now was completely alone. Pure energy waiting atop an ancient Aztec pyramid.

Waiting.

Waiting.

The sun burned down on the Silver Stretch.

The Highway Patrol discovered the abandoned limo about a week later. They were baffled. Not a sign of life could be found in or around her. Even the trunk was completely empty, seemingly wiped clean, yet she was idling and her gas gauge registered full.

When Harry Goldfind arrived to identify his stretch, he just shook his head. He couldn't figure it out. No one had seen or heard from Nate since the morning he'd left the Celeb lot for the Beverly Wood, but he never radioed in. According to Smitty, he never showed. Strange.

When the authorities questioned Smitty back at the Celeb offices, he played it extremely well. He, too, was plagued by the mystery of the missing driver.

"I can't figure it. He was Harry's top driver." He straightened his silk tie and brushed an infinitesimal speck of lint from his grey wool Sy Devore suit. "I'm new in the trade, but I've heard how guys burn out and leave the business without a word. Maybe he just flipped out."

With each of Smitty's lies, Celeb-10's motor would start and stop in the lot below. If you were close enough, you might have discerned the faint whirring sound of its motor echoing, "I'm here, Harry. It's me. Nathaniel."

But no one was close enough.

———— ◦《◉》◦ ————

After a year, Harry gave up trying to locate Nathaniel Kronstadt. He went ahead and bought the new Fleetwoods in the colors Nate had suggested--golds, burnished earth colors, but even with the new Fleetwoods, the old Silver Stretch was the best limo in the fleet. It ran like a top and never needed repairs.

Who would have believed that Nathaniel had metamorphosed into the only thing in this world he wasn't afraid to love? And Celeb-10 would keep Harry's company in the black for years and years. Like he'd always said to Nathaniel Kronstadt: "Go for the long dollar, Nate. The long dollar."

Hello, You've Reached Amy Byington

Amy Byington thought she'd taken care of all loose ends, leaving no unfinished business. A feeling of calmness filled her as she arranged copies of her cover letters by date in her search file. She methodically checked off each source on a log sheet stapled to the inside cover. She had spent the greater part of the morning and afternoon phoning each company, a final follow-up to her letters, before printing PASSED in large capital letters alongside the names of the companies who had filled the positions they'd advertised. Her final and most recent letter was to the personnel director at H. R. Morgan Company.

Amy stretched her long neck, thrusting her chin toward the ceiling. She could hear a small crackling inside her head. Years of working over files and typewriters had left her with what her chiropractor termed "a chronic occupational neck." She'd become adept at cracking it herself and felt a fresh surge of blood pulsate through her scalp. It was too late to contact the H. R. Morgan Company. Her kitchen clock read 5:00 P.M.

Ed Chalmers stared down at his hands and rubbed them together in an attempt to dry the perspiration that was leaving small blots on his desk. He found it difficult to look Amy Byington directly in the eyes, she'd been a loyal employee for nearly fifteen years. Personnel had tried their best to re-channel her within the company, but it was a matter of economics; the entire department was being scuttled. And Ed Chalmers had been given the pleasant task of telling his staff the news.

"With your experience and talent, you should have no difficulty finding another position. And if there is anything we can do to help, don't hesitate to ask." He handed her a pay envelope and letter of recommendation. "I'm sorry, Amy; I wish things were different. We'll miss you."

She rose and extended him her hand. It was hot. She felt her face flush and moisture began to bead across the ridge of her nose. "I understand, Ed. I'm sorry sales are down." She hesitated a moment, searching for something to say. Then she turned and left his office, closing the door behind her.

Amy reorganized her entire closet three times, weeding out things she no longer needed. She gave them to the Salvation Army. She honed in her budget and checked and rechecked her dwindling savings account.

The entire summer and early fall were spent job searching and putting her home files in order--insurance papers, pension funds, unemployment stubs, tax information--taking care of loose ends and unfinished business. It would be just a matter of time before one of the companies she had contacted would call her with an offer. Meanwhile, Amy enrolled in computer classes at her community college to enhance her work skills, signed on with several job agencies, and continued her search.

Nothing surfaced.

"Something will surface soon," she assured her mother during one of their ritual long-distance Sunday chats. "Don't worry. Everything is just fine. The boys are well, sassy and spoiled as ever. Give my love to Dad."

"I'm becoming a winter bear, conserving energy for the long months ahead," she thought out loud. Her two aging terriers became her constant companions. They took long walks together and watched the Chinese elm in front of the modest house she rented turn from a bright green to a laced bronze, dropping its small rusty leaves onto the cracked drive. They reminded Amy of little drops of blood. The rust spots stained the cement each fall, and she dutifully swept the fragile leaves into small piles and scooped them into the trash.

As the days grew shorter, Amy found herself sleeping longer and longer. The Chinese elm continued to spill its lacy bronze leaves onto the drive, and she gave up sweeping the little blood puddles into their customary mounds.

It had been six months since she was given notice, and nothing had surfaced. Amy's job search file had grown more than two inches thick.

Ed Chalmers's departing words played over and over inside her head: "You should have no difficulty in finding another position." What would she do? Unemployment was nearing the end, and her small savings was pushed to the edge. She certainly wouldn't dream of becoming a burden. She dismissed the thought, burden. She stretched and cracked her aching neck again.

"I'll phone the personnel director at H. R. Morgan tomorrow."

She gave her log one final appraisal before closing her search file.

"Get dressed, and I'll see you in my office."

Amy waited for Dr. Randolph to return from examining another patient in another of his examining rooms. She fidgeted with a small toy car on his oak desk.

"Well, Amy, you're in good health," Dr. Randolph said as he sat at his desk and checked her file. "Now, what's this problem with insomnia?"

"Probably just stress. I'm somewhat worried. You know, my job search and all ... it's made me a bit anxious. It's hard to sleep." She smiled.

He appraised his longtime patient and rubbed at his greying reddish beard. "That's understandable." He jotted something on his prescription pad. "This is a mild sedative. It should help you sleep." He tore the prescription from his pad, and she folded it into her purse. He laced his arm around her shoulder and walked her to his door. "Now, I want you to stop worrying and enjoy the holidays. Meanwhile, I don't have to see you for six months." Dr. Randolph gave his patient a reassuring hug.

"Thank you, doctor, and give my best to your family."

"Don't fret, Amy; something will surface soon.

Amy filled her prescription and stopped at a nearby nursery. She explained to the clerk about her Chinese elm and how she planned to liven its rusty look with year-long blooms around the base of its trunk. The clerk suggested impatiens and touch-me-nots. He sold her several flats and a large bag of humus, explaining how to till the soil and transplant the perennials all the while he carried the purchases to her car.

"Remember," he added. "Touch-me-nots need a lot of water,

and they'll give you color all year long."

Her terriers greeted her as though she'd been gone for years. She bent and patted her boys. "Tomorrow, my boys, you go to Dr. Santic for a while. I have a short trip ahead."

The two companions perked their ears and almost smiled at their mistress. The three had spent long years together and had been the best of friends.

She emptied her prescription into a blue glass container and held the apothecary jar up to the light. The yellow tablets appeared to be bright green inside the lovely blue jar.

Amy remembered to check her answering machine. There were no messages. She placed the flats of flowers and bag of humus at the base of the Chinese elm and then took her terriers on their last walk of the evening.

"Taking care of the year's unfinished business?" Dr. Santic asked as he examined Amy's terriers.

"Yes. I'm tying up loose ends. It's my last business trip for the year. I shouldn't be more than a week or ten days."

"Well, not to worry. We'll take good care of your boys."

Amy pulled a list from her purse. "This is just in case my trip goes longer than expected. I have some emergency numbers . . . my parents. They live out of town, but just in case there is an emergency, you can contact them."

Dr. Santic smiled. All the years he'd been her terrier's veterinarian, Amy was never gone longer than intended, yet, each time, she left him with her emergency lists and paid her boarding bills in advance.

"You're not planning on going to Alaska, are you?" he chided "You never can tell, Dr. Santic." Amy paid her bill in advance.

She spent the remainder of the afternoon sweeping up the

Chinese elm's blood puddles, mixing them into the humus. She aerated the soil at the tree base and spread the humus mix, just as the clerk from the nursery had advised. She then began to transplant her impatiens and touch-me-nots around the base of the elm trunk. Amy made certain to arrange each plant so its colors would blend into a pleasing spectrum to the eye--white, pink, orange, lavender, red, white, pink, orange--leaving an open space before transplanting the last of the lavender blooms from the final flat.

In it she placed her job search file, along with the empty prescription container. She planted the final lavender touch-me-not on top of her buried treasure, allowing enough humus mix beneath the plant for it to take root.

The transplanting took less than two hours, but it was time enough to give Amy the familiar jab in her long neck. She stretched her chin skyward toward the lacy elm's winter leaves until she heard the familiar crackle inside her head, and then she rose from her hands and knees and inspected her work. She encircled the Chinese elm and was delighted with her colorful efforts that danced around its trunk. The impatiens were just what the old tree needed, a burst of color and new life, a testament to renewal.

Amy was pleased.

There was a deep chill in the air, and she prepared for bed earlier than usual. She needed rest before her long trip. Amy turned on her answering machine, drank a full glass of water, and bundled under her quilt for a well-deserved rest. Her breathing became softer and softer. Like a winter bear, Amy slept and slept.

Night passed, and the early morning light shone through her bedroom window, shimmering off the blue apothecary jar resting on her bedside table.

The telephone rang.

Amy didn't rise to answer it.

"Hello. You've reached Amy Byington. I'm sorry I'm not here to take your call. Please leave your name and number, and I'll return your call as soon as possible."

BEEP.

"Hello, Amy. This is Meryl Jones, personnel director with H. R. Morgan Company. We received your letter and résumé in answer to our ad. We're very eager to see you in regard to the position we've advertised. Please call me at 897-22 . . . "

BEEP.

Amy Byington slept on and on while her touch-me-nots bloomed under the Chinese elm and the morning sun shone through the empty blue apothecary jar.

"Hello, you've reached Amy Byington . . . "

BEEP.

BEEP.

BEEP . . .

*By friendship you mean the greatest
love, the greatest usefulness, the
most open communication, the noblest
sufferings, the severest truth, the
heartiest counsel, and the greatest
union of minds of which brave men and
women are capable.*
- Jeremy Taylor. (1613-1667)

The Gift

Elizabeth was being led down an unfamiliar white corridor. Her heartbeat quickened with anticipation. What would she discover at the end of the corridor's thick lathed walls that led to the right? The corridor was ancient. Her red-haired guide flashed a quick slit-eyed glance back at her. She could tell by the young man's look that he was admonishing her for not keeping pace. They communicated by their eyes. No words were spoken, yet Elizabeth understood his every direction. His pale blue eye questioned her for stopping at a doorway to speak with an old, crippled man.

"Don't stop. You can't help him," her guide telegraphed.

She felt the crippled grey eyes burn through her. As she stretched her pale hand toward the old man, she realized that her red-haired guide had disappeared. "He must have taken the bend to the right," she blurted out loud. She hesitated for an instant.

"I'm sorry. I must keep up," she apologized to the old man

whose diseased eyes pleaded for help. "Don't worry; you'll be fine," she said. Panic rose inside her chest. Elizabeth was afraid to be alone in the corridor. She ran after her young guide. She listened to the sounds of her bare feet slapping against the cold cement and echoing back into her face. The racing patter of her feet became unbearably loud. Her heart sped up, and she grasped her long fingers against the icy curve of the corridor wall for support. She ran faster until her gauzy white nightgown entangled itself around her long legs, moist from the heat of the run. She nearly fell as she tripped over the front of the gown.

"Where is he? Where is he?" She cried out loud. Like a dancer, she regained her balance and rounded the corridor curve. Overwhelmed by a feeling of intense abandonment, Elizabeth realized that her pixie-eyed guide was nowhere in sight. Instinctively, she knew she needed him, as she saw that the corridor ended in a semicircular room a far distance ahead.

A group of strangers formed a cluster in the pink mist that hung in the corridor's circular end. Curiosity prodded her to approach the circle of strangers. As she neared, they turned and stared at her uninvited intrusion. Finally she could see who it was they were encircling, watching like birds of prey.

———※※※———

It was Sarah. Elizabeth saddened as she watched Sarah's wispy yellow hair sway back and forth, as she bobbed her head within the circle of strangers. Always the pleaser. The enchanted one. Elizabeth's sadness turned into rage as she watched her friend wobble and fall. "Why doesn't someone help Sarah to her feet?" she thought. Without thinking, she pushed into the crowd and swept Sarah into her arms. "My god, she is as limp as a Raggedy Ann doll. Airy as a little sparrow." As Elizabeth whisked Sarah up into her arms, Sarah took her lighted cigarette and snuffed out its ember with one swoop of her frail hand along the corridor floor. Elizabeth watched its bright red ember turn into a thin, white circle of smoke and disappear.

It had been three months since Sarah's funeral, and this was the first time that Elizabeth had dreamed about her childhood friend. She trembled as she disentangled herself from her sweat-drenched gown. She glanced at her bedside alarm. Its red, digital numbers flashed 4:00 A.M. Elizabeth watched through her Swiss white curtains as the smallest sliver of a waning moon cast its silver glow across her room. She swept her hand against her moist brow and brushed the tousled sandy hair from her face. She jumped up from her down-covered bed, lit a long brown cigarette, and began to pace back and forth in her room. Her dream had seemed so real. She couldn't stop thinking of Sarah. She pressed her palms to her mouth to cover the deep, animal sounds that swelled up from her deepest being. She couldn't stop crying. Elizabeth paced in her room until the silver light faded into lavender and turned into the glowing amber of 7:00 A.M.. It was time to get ready for work. Elizabeth knew that she should have called in "sick," but she'd become a workaholic since her divorce from Robert five years before. It was a luxury she couldn't afford. Sarah's death had made Elizabeth painfully aware of her own inner death, and she could no longer afford to ignore it. She had become the master of deception. Denial was her friend. She stared into the bathroom mirror at her puffy eyes. She brushed White Touch beneath them before adding the final touch of her make-up. Ready for work, she smiled her most convincing smile into the mirror and left.

It was Wednesday, May 22. Elizabeth made a mental note to straighten up her office cubicle as she shoved her briefcase beneath her desk at F. Feinstein & Associates, a celebrity clearing house that provided memorabilia for charitable and fundraising organizations. "I'll pick up a few plants at the market this evening," she thought as she performed her morning ritual of clearing the stacks of requests and putting them into neat priority piles. She was still sifting the files when the telephone rang.

"Is this Elizabeth Pearson?" A woman's breathless voice asked from the other end of the line.

"Yes, it is."

"You don't know the trouble I've gone through. You're the fifth person I've talked to, and I hope you don't give me the runaround," she said, impatiently.

"How can I help you?"

"My name is Minnie Johnson, and I represent the Band Boosters in Holesman, Wisconsin. We're having a celebrity auction a week from Friday. I've run into nothing but dead ends. You can't imagine how foolish I'll look to the rest of the committee. Can you send me anything?" She stopped to catch her breath.

"We represent many well-known celebrities. Don't worry. We'll be happy to send some things out." Elizabeth jotted down all of the pertinent information while the woman continued to go on and on for what seemed like eternity before hanging up. Elizabeth automatically scooped up biographical information on several celebrities and stuffed them into a manila envelope. She typed up the shipping request and attached it to the material. As she gathered the appropriate celebrities' photos to accompany the request, she stared down at one of them. "My God, my life has become an eight-by-ten glossy, and it's not even mine!"

"*Bonjour, mon chéri.*"

Elizabeth turned and smiled as Sarah glided, with a slight limp, into the rear entrance of the Bistro Gardens. "You look radiant."

The two friends embraced and waited for the maitre d' to seat them in the adjoining patio. "Your French lessons agree with you Sarah," Elizabeth said as they were seated at their table.

Heads turned from a nearby table, and Sarah exchanged pleasantries with a woman wearing a similar print. "Your dress is lovely. We have wonderful taste." The woman and her companions laughed.

"Isn't this the best?" Sarah winked at Elizabeth. "You look perfect in off-white. The rich always seem to wear white."

"Remember when we were in school and dreamed about coming to places like this?" Elizabeth smiled as she laced the crisp linen napkin across her lap.

Sarah reached her delicate hand across the table and patted Elizabeth's hand. "Trust me, *mon chéri*. Trust me."

Elizabeth tried not to stare at Sarah as their waiter took their order. She tried not to notice how thin her friend had become since their last luncheon. She tried not to let the pain of Sarah's progressive illness mirror in her face. Elizabeth was good at her job. She dealt with illness and tragedy every day. It was just a matter of sending out requests for charity fund-raisers, to listening to sad stories about illness and terminal diseases, diseases that she had never heard of, let alone understood, until she had gone to work for the celebrities' organization. She was good at blocking the pain, or so she thought, and here she was at the celebrated Beverly Hills restaurant having lunch with her dearest childhood friend. She tried to detect a sign, some indication that Sarah would acknowledge what was happening to her. Sarah, in her illness, was the stronger. She treated it as though she had broken a fingernail and had to rush to the nail salon for a slight repair. She was the bravest person Elizabeth had ever known.

The young waiter returned with their Chablis. Sarah was not reluctant to flirt, just the slightest. The young man was flattered as he poured their wine and disappeared. They raised their glasses in a toast.

"To us."

"Tell me about your trip. Tell me about England. About France."

The two women stared into each other's face. Years vanished and they were back in junior high school, sharing secrets at a slumber party.

"Paris is home. London wasn't so hot." Sarah sighed. Did I tell you that a taxi driver literally ran over my right foot in a roundabout? I looked down at my new red pumps and saw his tire tread permanently embossed across the top of my right shoe. My brand-new shoe! Thank God it wasn't my bad leg."

Elizabeth stared incredulously.

"Do you believe in reincarnation, Beth?"

Elizabeth pondered the question. She had studied metaphysics for years and was a bit reluctant to get into the subject. She knew that many skeptics attributed the philosophy to dotty ladies gathered around Ouija Boards.

She smiled. "Yes, I do Sarah."

A wide smile crossed Sarah's ethereal face. "So do I." She fluttered her small hands, drawing pictures in the air as she spoke. "So do I." Her face saddened just the slightest and she stared away for a moment before continuing. "When I was in Paris, particularly the countryside, I knew I was home. Strange, isn't it?"

Elizabeth shook her head. "Not really."

"Somehow, the language seemed to flow through me. I understood what people were saying. I know I've lived there before."

"And what about Paul? Does he want you to come back?"

Elizabeth realized that she had struck a sensitive chord. The last thing that she wanted to do was to add more pain.

Sarah drew herself up from her painful ribs. "He kissed my scars, Beth. He told me he loved me. He told me to study French when I returned home." Quickly, she changed her tone. Brash realism replaced her vulnerability. "But you know, *mon. chéri*, we're so different. Our lives, I mean. Paul is a perfectionist. And, me? Well . . . everything was lined in his closets to perfection. My make-up cluttered the commode. My clothes dropped to the floor, while his polished shoes lined up on racks like pristine soldiers. Oh, Beth, I love him, but in all reality, I'm such a slob and he's so . . . perfect."

Elizabeth stared down at the napkin laced across her lap. She knew what Sarah had said wasn't true. Sarah's home was immaculate. Sarah was perfection. If anyone was a slob, it was she, with her untidy office cubicle and her book- and paper-strewn apartment. She was always swearing to herself that she would organize her home and workplace. She was a pack rat, dragging junk around with her like Mother Courage.

"Sarah, you know you're not a slob."

Before Sarah could retaliate, their charming waiter placed their omelets *au fromage* and sautéed mushrooms on the table. Sarah blessed him with her most entrancing smile. He didn't notice her pain, as she drew herself up from her ribs again with a sigh. He was flattered by the attention.

"Enjoy," was all he said before leaving their table.

Elizabeth felt Sarah's pain. A ripple ran up her right shin. It felt like an electric jolt snapping away at the bone. "Oh, God, oh God."

Sarah dropped her facade. "I do love Paul, but I would be such a burden." She smiled and sipped her wine. "I know that I shouldn't smoke, dear Beth, but may I have one of your long, brown cigarettes? Please don't tell on me."

With reluctance, Elizabeth pulled a cigarette out from her red pack. "On one condition; if you eat your lunch first." She passed the cigarette to Sarah.

"Don't admonish me, Beth. It doesn't matter much now, does it? It would have been so easy to have gone for just a simple radical, but oh, no, I wanted to save . . . " She turned her attention to the adjoining table and the woman wearing the similar print. "It's a lovely restaurant, isn't it?" The woman and her companions nodded in agreement.

"Sarah, you're going to be fine." Elizabeth blurted out the sentence, hoping that saying it would make it so. She cut into her omelet. "Taste yours. It's scrumptious."

Sarah dabbled at her plate. "I want you to come out, but not until the house is finished. I want you to bring your tape recorder, as we'd planned. I have so many stories for you, Beth. For our book. But we can't record them until the house is finished. It will just be a few months more, and then we can talk about it. About our story."

Elizabeth panicked. "Sarah, I don't care if the house isn't

finished. I want to hear about you, about all of your travels. Let's not wait. I don't mind."

"No, *mon chéri*. The house is not ready. You work with celebrities all day long. You're the writer. I want our story to be ready when the house is ready. You're so impatient, *mon chéri*."

"Not really, Sarah," Elizabeth blurted out.

"I do believe in reincarnation," Sarah said with a sadness that pulled them both into the present. "Beth, the reason that I can't return to Paris and to Paul is because I need my medical insurance. You're right. I'm not such a slob."

Elizabeth grasped Sarah's hand. "I know."

"Be patient, Beth. It's just a few months longer. And wait until you see my Alvars. His stone lithographs are breathtaking. Vibrant oranges, yellows and burgundies. Life colors. I'm doing my room to match. Lately I spend a lot of time in my room, and there is still so much to do yet."

The two girlhood friends finished their lunch in silence. Finally Sarah looked up and smiled. She reached into her beige pocketbook and pulled out a long white envelope.

Elizabeth watched, not knowing what to make of it.

"I have a gift for you, Beth. It's not much, but I want to tell you about it now. Please open it."

Elizabeth hesitantly opened the long white envelope and unfolded a document. She began reading it, then caught her breath and set it down on the table.

"It's my will."

"Sarah, why are you showing this to me now?"

"Because I want you to use it for a trip. Beth, you never go anywhere. I love you, my friend, and this is the best gift that I can give you. I know you will use it well. I know you won't squander it. Use it for our story . . . I entrust this small legacy to your very capable hands, *mon chéri.*"

Elizabeth attempted to lighten the moment. "Well, that will be one hundred years from now."

"We still have time. The house is nearly finished. Promise me now, Beth, that you'll use it for a trip."

Elizabeth attempted to blink away the tears that welled in her eyes. "Oh, Sarah," was all that she could say.

Within three months from their luncheon at the celebrated Beverly Hills restaurant, Sarah's house had been completed and Sarah was gone. The cancer that had begun in her right breast metastasized, spreading into her back, her right hip, and finally into her liver. The terrible pain she had endured during her luncheon with Elizabeth had not stopped her from continuing to complete her home and leave her gift.

Throughout her final days in the hospital, Sarah had made it explicitly clear to friends to keep Elizabeth away. She wanted Elizabeth to remember her before the cancer had worn her exquisite body away, for Sarah's greatest legacy would be Elizabeth's gift, that special trip to enable her dear friend to tell their story, their camaraderie, their girlhood dreams, and the loves of their lives.

"Is this what you've been waiting for?"

Elizabeth looked up from her desk with a gasp. "Oh, Janet, you startled me."

Janet Carter playfully waved a white envelope across the desk and dropped it onto the celebrity's eight-by-ten glossy. "Well, aren't you just the least bit curious?" Janet teased as she paced in front of Elizabeth's desk, tapping her patent leather heel against the cold terrazzo floor. She could hardly contain her anticipation. Janet had seen the return address.

"It's from the conference."

"I know. Open it; I can't stand it!"

Elizabeth stared at the return address and then shook her head and grinned. "Now, don't get so excited. It's probably a nice rejection letter."

Janet grabbed the envelope from Elizabeth's hands and tore it open. "Now, will you please read it before I have a nervous breakdown?" She watched Elizabeth's eyes dart back and forth across the page as she read the letter in silence. "Tell me, what did they say?"

"I've been accepted. They've accepted me into the prose workshop. Janet, I made it. I can't believe it!"

"Hallelujah," Janet squealed. With one impetuous swoop, she scooped up a handful of request letters from the incoming basket and scattered them into the air.

Elizabeth felt suspended as she watched the stacks of mail waft into the air and then float and scatter across her office. "Janet, I just organized those this morning."

"Good. You can reorganize them after lunch. It'll give you something to do while you're planning your trip. When is the conference?"

"It starts in two weeks."

"Well, we'd better go down to Travel and place your airline ticket, don't you think?"

"After I fulfill this request."

Janet glanced down at the order. "The band boosters can wait until after lunch. Come on, Elizabeth; time is flying."

"I've told you everything about my friend, Sarah. Her gift has made this conference possible. Without it, I couldn't dream of going."

Janet shook her peppery hair and smiled. "I know, darlin'. The world thinks we're rich because we work for F. Feinstein & Associates. They think . . . " Her voice trailed off. She turned and hugged Elizabeth.

"I wish Sarah could be here to see the letter, to know that I will be going to the conference."

"Who said that she isn't?" Janet said with reverence. "Are you going to write about her?"

"What do you think?"

"I think that I don't want to see your face around here for the next two weeks. And I think Sarah knows." Janet scooped up a few pieces of remaining mail and tossed it into the incoming basket. "Now, let's head downstairs to Travel and, on our way, we can decide where to go for lunch."

Elizabeth waited in the baggage area at Reno, Nevada airport. She realized that she had over packed, as she glanced down at her three bulging suitcases. She retrieved her instructions from her purse and reread them. "A guide will meet you at the airport to drive you from Nevada to the California side of Lake Tahoe and Olympic Valley."

"Hi, I'm David. Are you Elizabeth Pearson?"

"Yes," Elizabeth said nervously.

"Good, you're my charge!" With that, the exuberant young man swept up her luggage. "Follow me."

Elizabeth felt the blast of the hot Reno air hit her face as she trailed after David into the airport parking lot. "This is my first writers conference," she said, as if to apologize.

"I can tell. You over packed. You'll love it. It's my second." David piled her suitcases into the back of his jeep. "I'm on scholarship; that's why I'm picking you up. You pay my way this year, so to speak."

Elizabeth couldn't help noticing his striking red hair as they sped along the highway in the direction of the Sierras.

"You're from Los Angeles, huh?"

"Yes, I am."

"You won't miss it. Stay here for a week, and you'll never want to go back. Believe me. It happens to all of us."

Elizabeth became entranced by the scenery. She snapped pictures the entire way as David drove through the mountains. She held on for dear life as he whipped his jeep onto the side road that led into Squaw Valley and the community of writers.

David screeched to a dusty halt in front of the geodesic dome that housed the theater and offices. "Here we are," he announced. "Go on in and register, and then I'll take you up to your condo."

Elizabeth nodded to several other registering writers as she entered the main office. She returned to David's jeep carrying sheaves of paper.

"Your schedule, huh?" David quipped.

"Yes. My story is first up tomorrow."

"Good, my charge. You'll get it over with first off. That way, the pressure will be off and you can really get down to some serious writing. Where are you staying?"

"Condo number eight, on Christy Lane."

"Hold on, charge." David gunned his motor and sped across the bridge, crossing the creek, passing the grocery store, and heading up winding Christy Lane. He screeched the jeep to a halt in front of a white, tri-level condo nestled in the pines. David unloaded Elizabeth's suitcases and piled them onto the wooden porch. "Do you want me to carry them down?"

"That's okay." She couldn't take her eyes away from his vibrant red hair. "Are you Irish?"

"How can you tell?" He grinned.

"I guess your hair gives you away."

David laughed. "The last name's O'Rourke. That's about as Irish as one can get." He jumped back into his jeep. "I'll see you at the orientation, and then dinner at Le Chamois. Remember, the orientation starts at six o'clock sharp."

"I'll see you then, David." Elizabeth braced herself before entering condo number eight.

She could hear muffled sounds of laughter and conversation drifting up from the downstairs living room. Elizabeth grasped her thin hand along the thick, white lathed banister as she descended the stairs into the group of seven strangers, other nervous writers who would be her housemates for the next two weeks and eventually her friends.

"Hello, my name is Elizabeth Pearson," she said.

The circle of strangers opened. The people smiled and began introducing themselves. Sarah's image flashed before her eyes, just for an instant, inside the circle of strangers. It all seemed so familiar. This was Elizabeth's dream. Elizabeth felt instantly at home. Sarah, in her death, had given her a most precious gift.

Elizabeth knew that Sarah had foreseen the conference, a safe place for her to be able to write, and now Elizabeth would be able to tell Sarah's story, their stories. Elizabeth's trip to the conference was indeed Sarah's greatest gift of all.

Calamity is the perfect glass wherein we truly see
and know ourselves.
- Sir William Davenant(1606-1668).

The Solution

The fires had taken everything. The sky was ablaze with red and orange embers being whipped up by the powerful Santa Anas that were moving north from Los Angeles. Blue vapor rose from the charred pines silhouetted against the grey horizon. Wildlife had long fled the inferno. Creek beds were full of ash and dead fish, their eyes boiled white in a permanent glaze.

Christina crawled along the black asphalt road threading through the deserted landscape. The acrid smell pierced her surgical mask. Tears spilled from her watering eyes. Black streaks dripped down her mask, creating an eerie ghostlike face.

She then lay prone on the road, trying to get her bearings. Robert was no longer in sight, and she feared he was lost. Suddenly a bright light shone a few feet ahead and a small child seemed to appear from nowhere. The child held out her hand and offered a key.

Christina turned her gaze toward Justine. The beautiful fair-haired child smiled down on her pitiful follower and motioned for Christina to take the last of the three pewter keys that hung from the large ring she was extending in her left hand. Christina's journey had been long. Everything she loved had been taken away. She was alone with only the angelic Justine, a mere child, offering the last key to . . . ? "It is a sign; it must be," Christina thought.

Justine smiled and nodded. "You are right, Christina. It is a sign. I've come to you before, in your dreams. The sky is burning as the prophets had warned. The decision is in your hands."

Slowly, Christina pulled herself up from the asphalt road that had begun to melt beneath her. A decision must be made, or she would be sucked into the melting quagmire. She ran her bloodied hands through her tangled, russet hair while continuing to stare at the beautiful, angelic Justine, whose eyes would not leave hers.

The child's pink and blue cotton dress wafted with the winds that had changed their pull from the north. Christina squinted as the burning clouds became ever brighter. She turned to look behind at what she was leaving. There was nothing but emptiness. Desolation. The asphalt road popped into flames, encroaching from a close distance behind her. She stood on a precipice. The flames were approaching rapidly from the south, and Justine held out the last of the three keys before her.

An ancient memory reverberated inside of Christina's head. Its voice was thunderous. "In life, you must remember there are only three keys. Nothing else matters. Your earthly path will lead you through many experiences, many choices, many decisions, but remember, my beloved novitiate, only three keys are of importance. They are Love, Peace, and Charity. All others are mere diversions that will play with your heart and soul. You will be tested many times. I will come to you again and again during your search. I will come to you in dreams. I will come to you in the guise of others. I will test you, for I am you."

Christina smiled at Justine. The child had made her remember. Christina reached out her bloodied hand and took the final key that Justine thrust out to her.

It was the key of Love.

Fame is an undertaker that
pays but little attention to
the living, but bedizens the dead,
furnishes out their funerals, and
follows them to the grave.
- Charles Caleb Colton. (1780-1832)

Do You Know Marcus Hanley?

It was Indian summer in Los Angeles. Steam rose in visible swirls from the asphalt pavement along Sunset Boulevard. Marcus Hanley choked on the heat as he parked his white Bentley in its allotted space beneath his office towers.

Labor Day was gone; school had begun, and Marcus was going through the ritual of another Monday morning at his own Marcus Hanley Productions. He would be thirty-five the following week, and he had arrived. A self-made millionaire in the volatile music industry, Marcus had bypassed his usual Brooks Brothers pinstripe for a faded blue work shirt and jeans.

This Monday morning struck him as unusual, eerie. A chill rushed up his spine as he passed through the lobby and rode the elevator to the fourteenth floor. He was not with his body. His mind was elsewhere. The recent pain of his brother's death and funeral still dug at the pit of his stomach. Work had eased the pain for Marcus before.

The elevator doors whooshed open, depositing the handsome sandy-haired entrepreneur onto the fourteenth floor. Secretaries and staff scurried when they saw their boss heading toward the double inlaid ebony doors that separated his kingdom from the rest of his offices.

It was the place where deals were consummated and careers were launched or aborted. His staff members were polite, nodding as he swept past them. One could barely discern his slight limp. Childhood polio had left his right leg a bit weak.

"My God." It seemed like yesterday to Marcus, trying to talk his brother out of volunteering for a nightmare with no purpose. Rage burned inside his temples. "Why didn't the little jerk let me buy him out?" he thought. "Why did David think he was on some damn mission?"

Marcus sat at his designer desk and glanced at the neatly stacked documents awaiting his signature. He stared straight ahead at the closed doors separating him from the rest of the world. "Why, why, why?"

Although most people were aware of David's delayed stress syndrome and pretended it was his problem, a few were legitimately shocked to learn Marcus's younger brother had put his .45-caliber keepsake to his own temple and methodically pulled the trigger. A few key people from the office had attended the funeral. Jenny, Marcus's personal secretary, had taken up an office collection, and the appropriate wreath bearing the perfect inscription was delivered to the gravesite by the top limousine service in town. It was an incident not to be brought up in polite circles, yet it had happened, and like good professionals, staff members handled their boss's tragedy with decorum.

Marcus hated the finality of death. Life was precious to him. Now he felt like a helpless victim, caught on a black treadmill. What could he have done to change the script? Oh, if only to change the events! He held the power to make or break an artist's career with the elegant brush of his black felt-tip pen, yet like an abandoned child, he faced the reality of his loss for the first time.

He pushed back into the soft fabric of his chair and stared past the exquisite decorated office, through the black-tinted glass secluding the fourteenth floor from the Los Angeles streets below. Encased in a solitary glass obelisk that housed the crème de la crème of the music business, the weaver of dreams wanted to run away. He wanted to hide. Marcus wanted out.

The telephone rang several times before he heard it. Intuitively, he knew that it was Rachel. Her honey-soft voice warmed the chill that was enveloping him. Rachel knew him well, and Marcus realized how much he loved and needed her. They were talking about their trip to the cabin in the mountains when he heard muffled voices beyond the double doors an instant before they flew open. Before he could register shock, three .25-caliber bullets pierced his chest, thrusting him hard against the soft decorator chair. The receiver dropped from his hand, with the muffled sound of Rachel's voice screaming from the dangling instrument.

A solitary tear gathered in the corner of his right eye and began to slowly flow down the angular slope of his chiseled cheekbone. He made a thrusting attempt for the receiver that hung beyond his grasp. If he could just reach his lifeline to Rachel, he would be safe.

Veins began to well atop his graceful hand, pulsating blue against his already white, cold flesh. He felt his body heat condensing as it traveled methodically upward toward his head. There was no pain, only tiny, electric pings that left a trail of numbness on their ascent.

Incredibly bright colors flashed into an instantaneous spectrum of a rainbow, and as if a prism were directing them, they transformed themselves into sparkling white dots of luminous light that swam in his watering eye. The myriad sensations took only an instant from first impact, as Marcus's brain began its dielectric dance.

From inside his body he watched his lone tear continue its descent until it transformed itself into frothy, bubbling caps that foamed atop cresting waves. Rachel's plaintive cries transmitted themselves along telephone cables to Marcus's fourteenth floor suite and then ebbed and dissolved into the lapping sounds of the sea.

Within moments following the impact, Marcus was out of his body, traveling back in time. He found himself transported to the sands in front of his mother's weathered beach house, standing dried and bleached like the bones of a dead whale that had given up its flesh to the elements.

It was the house where Marcus and his younger brother David were born, the house where Clara Hanley had raised her sons, alone, after their father had walked out on the family one September morning and never returned.

The salt air cut through the house's proud, white exterior where once brilliant green shutters hung stationed at the front window. Some of the slats had fallen away, and the faded shutters were in need of paint and repair. Clara's gnarled wicker rocker sat on the fading grey deck. Her clay-potted Martha Washingtons lined the porch railings, and their torrid shades of pink and red blooms gave testament to passersby that life was still very much in progress at the Hanley house.

Marcus felt the ocean mist and smelled the pungent sulfur aromas floating along the Santa Monica coastline. He stretched out on his towel, and its deep pile pressed into his bare back. Alone, with only the sounds of the sea and gulls, he soaked in the healing warmth of the sun. It eased the ache in his right leg, the sole, faint mark on his seemingly perfect, slender physique.

In the distance, Marcus heard the sound of approaching roller skaters licking across the hot pavement. He knew that the boys were on their way, and a knowing smile crossed his lips.

Staccato licks of metal skates bit into a hot, white pavement. Echoing boys' laughter cut through still sea air. Even the lazy gulls took notice and swirled up from the hot, yellow sands into the aquamarine sky on that sultry June afternoon, several months back in time.

Twelve-year-old Jimmy pumped his electric-blue bicycle pedals for all they were worth. His sun-bleached hair hung in paintbrush swipes across a twisted orange sweatband that hugged his tanned forehead. He sucked in the sea air while his eight-year-old brother, Binky, clung on from behind, scrunching up his freckled nose and shrieking in mock fright.

Tim, their ten-year-old pal and Santa Monica's skateboard champ, maneuvered alongside the bicyclers, swerving in and around with lanky surfer expertise. Their yips and howls rang down the strand in boyish bravado.

Daredevils cutting across pavements, the trio became fast racers in the Indianapolis 500, imagining the crowds. The hot smell of oil and gasoline cut into summer skies, when suddenly something caught Binky's eye, and he lurched off the back of Jimmy's electric-blue bike.

"He's here! Oh boy, oh boy, he's here!" Binky screamed.

Jimmy and Tim came to a reverent halt.

All three boys stared at Marcus Hanley's white Bentley parked at the curb. It shone in the afternoon sunlight, a luminous jewel in contrast to the withered, white clapboard house that had seen many summers.

"Wowee, he's here! Marc is here," Binky shrieked in excitement.

"How 'bout keepin' your loud mouth shut, Bink?" Jimmy said with a hiss. "Someone in the house just might see you foolin' around Marcus's car."

Binky hated it when his brother reminded him that he wasn't in charge. "Aw, I was just lookin', Jimmy."

Jimmy's stern face softened just a hair. "Well, look, but keep it down," he warned. He motioned the two boys to follow his lead, and the ragtag soldiers made their way alongside the Hanley house toward the back fence that split the strand from the beach.

Slowly, Jimmy and Tim pulled themselves up the fence. A loose board flipped hard against Tim's right big toe. "Owww! Geezus, my toe. I cut my dumb toe," he wailed. He hopped to the ground and shot a wild punch at the culprit. "That'll show ya! Cheap fence!"

Binky let out an uncontrolled giggle. He swallowed it hard when Jimmy shot him the Evil Eye.

"Will you guys keep it down, for crying out loud?"

"I didn't do it on purpose. What do ya think, I cut my dumb toe on purpose?" Tim bleated. He ripped the orange bandanna from his forehead and tied it across his injured toe.

Jimmy ignored him and turned his gaze across the top of the fence. He spotted Marcus lying near the water's edge. He stared. Marc was his hero, too. He just didn't want to let onto the others.

He didn't like the feeling of looking silly, like some star-struck kid. After all, he was the oldest of the three.

The boys hung on the fence and secretly watched their hero sleeping alone on the beach.

Clara Hanley paced in her dining room, arranging and then rearranging her beautifully laid table. She brushed a wisp of graying blond hair from her eyes and straightened her floral chintz dress. Her frail, spotted hands darted like moths from one elegantly placed piece of heirloom china to the next on her hand-crocheted ecru tablecloth. She fiddled with the cut glass spice and condiment holders and then folded and re-folded her best linen napkins that she had painstakingly drawn through her prized tortoise shell napkin rings. She pulled at a straying wisp of hair and neatly folded it, with a long hairpin, into the double braids crisscrossing the top of her small head.

The sound of the slamming fence board drew her to the side window. Clara peered through her frayed screen and spotted the three boys hanging on her back fence like fledgling sparrows, legs dangling, peering toward their hero. She turned to her younger son, David. Strong and athletic in build. not at all like his older brother. "Where's your brother?" she questioned, attempting to mask the strident rasp in her throat that belied the fear she was trying to hide.

"Still on the beach, I guess," David replied, smiling at his agitated mother. Like a mischievous boy, he whisked a green olive from a cut glass condiment dish and popped it into his mouth.

"That's just like him. Invite him for the weekend so he can talk some sense into your foolish head, and what does he do? Spends all of the time lolling in the sun."

"C'mon, Mom; Marc isn't my keeper. I can make my own

decisions." David was about to pop another olive, when Merrilee appeared from the kitchen and set a honey-glazed ham in the center of the beautiful awaiting table.

Merrilee curtsied and playfully swept her long, summer-sunned from her face. She gave David a seductive wink and let down one shoulder of her peasant blouse. They were very much in love. Suddenly her mood switched. "I don't understand you. Talk to him. He has connections," she said somberly.

"Connections, huh?" He pulled her onto his lap. "You make him sound like some shady underworld figure."

"Oh, David, stop making light of the situation. I'm serious." She pouted as she pulled away from her fiancé.

"So am I," he replied. He gazed at her as she continued her pout, before turning and disappearing into the kitchen. David held the back of his muscular neck between his squared, tanned hands and tried to press away the tension that his decision was causing. He turned his gaze through the frayed window screen toward Marcus lying on the beach. David stared, and his mind took him back to the days they were children.

David was five years old. He shrieked when the surf licked at his small legs. The sticky seaweed washed up in the afternoon tide and swirled about his ankles. He ran toward the sandcastle he and Marcus had made, to shore it up before the incoming tide washed away their efforts. Dropping to his knees, he furiously pressed the soft, moist sand into protective mounds with the palms of his tiny hands.

Eight-year-old Marcus called for David to wait, as he hobbled toward the water's edge. He continued his limping gait, when suddenly his braced leg caught on a clump of seaweed. Marcus's frail arms spun like whirligigs, causing his spindly body to flail and lose control. The downward momentum toppled the delicate child square into the sandcastle. Furious and humiliated, Marcus grabbed the first thing in sight, a toy soldier that had toppled onto the leveled sandcastle. Without thought, David's toy soldier went hurtling, striking David's forehead with a bullet-cracking thud.

David wailed and grabbed his wound. Blood trickled between his pudgy baby fingers. Shocked, Marcus stretched out a hand, but his ugly metal brace grounded him to the spot. Before he could reach David, he felt two powerful hands yank him skyward from the heap and then smack him hard across his face. Both boys bellowed.

"It was an accident, Daddy!" David recalled his brother's cries, and then the memory faded.

The session was in progress at Record City Recording Studios. Jerry Goldman paced in the state-of-the-art, high-tech control booth. He nervously brushed his salt-and-pepper-colored hair off his tanned forehead as he adjusted his tinted aviator glasses. The record company brass watched like carrion worms as their chief of Artist and Repertoire slowly lost his cool.

Jerry checked the wall clock. Its hands were nearing 4:00 P.M. Marcus was exactly one hour late. Sales were slipping, and Jerry's department was shouldering the blame.

"Why on earth is Marcus holding up the date?" he wondered to himself. "Damn, my future hangs on this deal." He shot a quick smile toward the three executives seated unceremoniously on the sumptuous guest divan.

This was Sunday afternoon, and the brass had given up their routine racquetball/tennis/Sunday barbecue to be there, and it was obvious that the three executives weren't too happy to be kept waiting by the fair-haired wunderkind. The three tennis-garbed men grudgingly gave up their "day of rest" to get back into the fast lane. Sundays were their day away from the treadmill, booze, and hangers-on, and, for all they cared, the hot new discovery could wait until Monday.

Jerry nodded to the engineer to lay down a rough track on "The September Reign." Five young musicians adjusted their kaleidoscopic World War II costumes, strutted their best macho dance, and aced themselves up to knock "the old men" off their chairs. This was their big break. This was THE BIG TIME., and Marcus Hanley was late.

"Where in the hell is he?" Jerry thought as he motioned to the group to start their countdown. One hundred and ten decibels rocked through the massive JBL speakers and careened into the control booth. The blitz was on!

Napalm oozed across the thatched roofed village like the bubonic plague. Its jellied flames engulfed the terrified women and children, who lunged desperately for the Vietnamese paddies to quench the fire that was enveloping them. Their anguished cries rose with the acrid smell of burning flesh and disintegrating bones.

Three young American soldiers blasted through the crimson village, shooting jellied destruction from their smoking, hand-held cannons.

The gulls swirled out to sea on that sultry Sunday afternoon many months ago. Marcus awoke from his nightmare with a lurch, causing an excruciating spasm to ripple down his right side. The pain pierced his leg, and he let out a cry. The gulls fluttered up from the sand once more and flew out to the calmness of the sea.

The boys scrambled across the Hanleys' back fence and made

a dart down the sand toward their hero.

Binky took the lead. He loved Marcus and wanted to be just like him when he grew up. Marcus always gave them his newest 45 single releases, and it made Binky feel special to all of his friends.

Clara Hanley watched the four from her window. She fluttered her delicate hands above her taut braids. "Oh, God," she thought, "please talk David out of volunteering for the draft. Please, please," she pleaded silently under her breath. "David is the last of the line." She turned away from the window to answer the echoing telephone.

Jerry Goldman held admiration and respect for Clara Hanley, and he valiantly tried to hide his anxiety from her. He whispered into the receiver from the studio control booth, "Mrs. Hanley, I'm sorry to bother you." He cleared his throat, while he felt the three executives' stares penetrating his shoulder blades. "We've been . . . uh, expecting Marcus. He wouldn't be at your house, would he?" Jerry flashed an "I've got it covered" smile at the irritated brass.

Clara sighed. "He's on the beach," she relayed. "I'll have him call you when he gets back to the house." She didn't wait for Jerry's goodbye. She just let down the receiver into its cradle and went back to her side window. Another Sunday dinner would be spoiled. She was used to it with Marcus, yet she always held the hope that he would stay and share a meal. She had tried to make it up to him in so many ways for waiting so long to take him to the doctor that epidemic polio summer. Clara had always blamed herself, and food was love. Sunday dinners were her way of making up for not knowing. She had always attributed Marcus's aloofness as scorn for her, when in reality, it never was. He was a loner, and Clara never understood that.

The three boys crowded around Marcus's Bentley, in anticipation of the wonderful surprises awaiting them on his rare visit to the house on the Strand.

Marcus loved it. "Here, guys, these are promos. Make sure you tell your buddies to go out and buy them."

"I will, I will," Binky yelled. He grabbed a handful of records and ran down the street. He could hardly wait to brag to his friends.

Jimmy and Tim kept their cool. "Thanks a lot," they said.

"You've got it." Marcus watched the boys disappear down the street until the electric blue bicycle blended with the horizon and the staccato licks of the skateboard wheels melded with the sound of the Santa Monica surf.

Later on, the cool water felt good on Marcus's hot skin.

David leaned against the vanity while his brother showered. "You know, this whole thing has been set up so that you'd talk me out of enlisting."

Marcus turned off the water and wrapped a towel around his waist. "Yeah, Mom never was too subtle, but she's right. It's suicide for you to enlist. They'll send your handsome butt to Nam. Don't think it's some kind of a picnic, David."

"What would you have me do?" David snapped. "Your polio kept you out."

Marcus winced at the words and then continued to dress. He stopped and looked hard at his brother. "Want a job? Want me to fix it so you would be the only visible support for Mom?" He continued to glare at his naive brother. "It can be done, you know."

"Yeah, I know you've got connections." David sighed. "But I'm not interested in the music business. No offense, Marc."

"I thought you were the pacifist. What happened to your interest in the ministry?" Marcus blurted out, going for the guilt as his ace card.

"It goes with me," David replied calmly.

"Oh, David, don't be so damn naive. You know as well as I it's an economic bloodbath over there. You'd do yourself and everyone concerned one big favor by staying home. Martyrs are dead people." He shot his brother a scornful look.

Merrilee poked her pretty face into the doorway.

"Don't you believe in knocking?" Anger welled beneath Marcus's controlled voice.

"Jerry Goldman is on the phone. It's the third time he's called, Marc." She gave David a "what's going on?" look. He avoided the question in her eyes. She hesitated a moment before mustering up her most impish smile. "Dinner is ready."

Marcus brushed the top of her head with a brotherly kiss. "Tell Mom thanks, but I'm late for a session."

"Now, Mom, you don't want me to get fired, do you?" Marcus smiled as he pressed two crisp, fifty-dollar bills into Clara Hanley's small hand. He curled her tiny knuckles into a boxer's fist and brazed it across his chin in a mock punch.

Clara Hanley offered a resigned smile as she watched Marcus speed away in his white Bentley.

David opened the screen door behind her. "Come on in, Mom; your pretty table is waiting."

Clara sighed and entered the open door.

Jerry Goldman gave a start when he felt Marcus's hand touch his shoulder. Seeing him, Jerry smiled and relaxed. Marcus addressed the three disgruntled executives. "How's it going, guys?" He smiled.

"Great."

"Couldn't be better."

"Looks like we got a smash for the company."

"Glad to hear it." Marcus turned back to Jerry, whose blue-grey eyes were beginning to water behind his tinted aviators. "May I?" Marcus asked, indicating the producer's seat at the control board.

"Oh, sure, Marc, sure," Jerry said. He rose hesitantly from the producer's spot. He shifted casually to the side of the controls, crossed his arms, and leaned against the thick, brown corduroy wall. He stared straight ahead through the double-pane glass where The September Reign was tuning up, preparing for the "real take."

Marcus slid into the seat next to the engineer, who nodded and adjusted the controls. "What do you think?"

"They've got some good tunes. One's a sure monster." The engineer shot Marcus a cunning grin. "They could be as big as The Stones."

Marcus smiled and turned to Jerry. "Jer, I could sure go for a burger. Do you mind?"

"No, not at all." Jerry was taken off balance. This date was his baby.

"Thanks. Get yourself something, too."

"That's okay. I'm not hungry." Considering his delicate situation, Jerry knew that Marcus's request was an instant anathema, as far as his career with the company was concerned. He avoided the three executives' eyes as he made a hasty exit.

Marcus pressed the intercom and announced, "Take one, The September Reign. 'Everything's Gonna Be All Right.'"

The drum roll bounced off the speakers and, just for an

instant, Marcus's nightmare flashed before him.

The three soldiers blasted their napalm into the studio and then disappeared as the group's music built-in crescendo.

He would have to deal with David's problem later. This group was the vehicle that would get him up the mountain.

The three executives watched from their spot on the divan.

"See no evil."

"Speak no evil."

"Hear no evil."

They had a "hot act," or so they thought!

"Everything's Gonna Be All Right" sounded even better on Marcus's own Technics playback unit. The music encircled him as he sat the midpoint in his home entertainment center. He had all of the latest equipment at his fingertips. The elegant, color-coordinated room looked like a recording studio. He smiled to himself. "Fantastic. It's a hit."

The entry intercom rang. It was Jerry.

Marcus let him in. "What took you so long?"

"I had to stop for gas." Jerry sighed. "God, it's nearly midnight. I'm exhausted." He slumped into a chair, pushed back his aviators, and rubbed at his watery, blue-grey eyes.

Marcus turned off the music.

"That should set the company on its ear." Jerry smiled. "Being in this business almost twenty-five years teaches you something about predicting a winner when you hear one."

"They're not getting the group," Marcus stated calmly.

"What?" Jerry was in shock, complete disbelief. He absolutely knew that this would be the end of his career. He'd be canned for sure.

Marcus simply smiled his enigmatic smile. "Trust me, trust

me," was all that he said.

"Trust me, we know what we're doing," the young, black paramedic snapped.

Jerry blanched white with fear as he watched the paramedic team scurrying around Marcus's limp, bleeding form slumped behind the desk in his fourteenth floor suite.

Scuffling and hysteria continued outside of the double doors.

Jenny attempted to reassure Rachel on her own phone. "Everything is going to be all right," she said, shakily.

The black paramedic hooked Marcus into the portable life-monitoring system.

Marcus's pulse registered weakly. His eyes remained open, but there was a lifeless glaze across them. An IV was inserted into a protruding vein atop his right hand. Marcus emitted a low, drowning sound from the center of his being. His eyes rolled back, and he sucked for air.

"Damn it, we're losing him!" the black paramedic yelled. "Get ready for CPR!" He made a fist with both hands and thrust a whacking thud to the center of Marcus's limp chest.

The reality of the lifesaving technique was too horrible for Jerry to stomach. He turned toward the wall and began to weep. The black paramedic continued to pound Marcus's chest.

Marcus felt nothing, yet his ears registered the sound of the whacking thuds. His life's blood began to trickle from his right nostril. He stared straight ahead. The thuds transmitted him into another memory.

Jack Feinman slammed his fist hard against the top of the polished conference table. The company's chief executive officer was furious. "What in the hell do you mean, we're not getting The

September Reign?" He shot an icy glare across the table directly into Marcus Hanley's eyes.

Marcus lowered his head for an instant, while the other three executives followed Feinman's stare.

Jerry Goldman adjusted his aviator glasses and nervously fumbled with a loose shirt button.

The air hung heavily for what felt like eternity. Finally, Marcus broke the silence. "If you gentlemen would be so kind as to read the agreement, you'll see that The September Reign has always been under contract to Marcus Hanley Productions. I paid for their session, not the company. It appears that no one bothered reading the fine print."

All eyes shifted to Jerry Goldman, their chief of A & R. The writing was on the wall. Jerry knew that it was just a matter of time before he would be out the door, except there was one hitch. Being the dedicated corporate man that he was, Jerry failed to have a trump card up his sleeve.

Marcus rose and courteously excused himself. The door had barely closed behind him when Jack Feinman went into his eleventh-hour rage. "No hard feelings! That bastard," he bellowed. The arteries on his neck swelled into fire hoses. "If that snot nose thinks he can pull one over on the company, he's in for one helluva shock. I'll personally see to it that he fails." The meeting formally adjourned.

Rachel Allen had been waiting in Jerry's office for nearly an hour. The diminutive brunette songwriter knew the ins and outs of the business. She'd delivered a string of hits over the years for Jerry and the company, and she knew that he never kept her waiting for an appointment unless it was crucial. She sensed trouble when he appeared and apologized for the wait.

Jerry hugged her. "It's been too long. Welcome home. It agrees with you."

"Thanks, it's good to be back." She laughed, causing her strikingly handsome face to crinkle into pixie dimples. "You warned me about trekking off to Colorado in search of 'The Mountain.'"

"Somehow, Rachel, I never saw you as the rancher's bride."

"Well, you can't blame a girl for trying." The recent pain bubbled beneath her calm demeanor. "Anyway, I was lucky enough to get my place in the Glen back."

"I'm glad. You did your best work there." He winked with affection.

"Of course, you'll have to fill me in on who's who in the fast lane."

"You'll pick up the track in five minutes. Now, what do you have for me?"

Rachel put her cassette on the deck and turned up the volume.

Jerry leaned back in his chair and was overwhelmed by the richness of the music that cascaded into his office. Tributaries melted into rivers and echoed through canyons. He looked at his friend and knew that she'd come home, bringing her experience of the mountains with her.

After the uproar with Feinman, Marcus was putting the last of his personal effects into his attaché case when the phone rang. It was Merrilee. "Where are you?" she scolded. "David's plane is taking off in an hour. You promised that you'd see him off."

"Sorry for the delay." He sighed. "I'm on my way." He glanced at the gold and platinum albums bolted to his office wall. He knew that he had left the company a small legacy during his three-year tenure.

"Nothing is forever," he thought as he closed his door behind him.

Marcus slipped down the hall past Jerry's office. He'd call him from home and explain everything in detail. Right now he had to make LAX in time to see David off. "There's a million ways to commit suicide," he thought as he rushed past the familiar faces of his peers and hurried down to the guard's station and parking lot in the rear of the company complex.

Richie North stopped him before he was able to get into his white chariot. "Hey, Marcus Hanley, remember me?" He pushed all five-foot two of himself into Marcus's face.

Marcus knew it was rude, but he couldn't help staring at Richie North's open-to-the-navel Hawaiian shirt and fake gold chains that were turning his perspiring chest a dull green.

The over-the-hill singer did his best "tap dance." He'd lost too many battles and had seen too many Amateur-Night-Hollywood-Get-Discovered-Toilets. Deep within his dyed hair and "you don't stand a chance, Charlie," life, Richie knew that if someone in the upper stratosphere of the business would just give him a break, he would show all of those back-home folks who'd laughed in his face and told him to keep pumping gas that he was somebody. If just one executive in that rarified world would give him the nod, he would throw the laughter back into those creeps' faces. He would get the girl that everyone fantasized about, whomever she may be. Richie North thrust out his tape. "Remember me? You caught my gig last month at The Bitter West. Remember me?"

Marcus Hanley remembered Richie North. And he didn't remember him. He stared straight into the sad man's brown eyes. "Yeah, The Bitter West. I remember you," he lied.

Richie North lit up and glowed. "Here's my tape, man.

Remember? You said to put my songs on tape."

Marcus knew that he'd never make it to LAX in time to see David off if he kept up the producer act. Knowing full well he'd never see the singer again, he said, "Drop it with the guard. He'll get it to my office. I'm late, man. You understand."

"Oh, yeah, sure. Sure, Mr. Hanley. Thanks, thanks a lot." Richie North nearly tripped as he rushed toward the guard's station.

"God bless the poor guy," Marcus thought as he jumped into his Bentley and sped away.

He wished that he'd had wings. David would be in Texas before Marcus could make the airport. With the escalation in Vietnam and military carriers working overtime twenty-four hours a day, the government was shipping personnel to their ordered destinations by commercial carriers. David's orders were to report to Fort Bragg. "Damn, I wish Rapid Transit would make it just once on the ballot," he thought aloud as he careened down the San Diego Freeway. He hated LAX, with its infernal roundabout traffic snarls.

When he finally pulled in front of the TWA terminal, he had ten minutes to spare before David's plane took off. "What the hell," he thought as he left the Bentley in a passenger loading zone. The parking ticket would be worth it.

Marcus ran past Baggage Claim and zipped through the security checkpoint. Now it was the five-minute-mile dash down the mosaic hallway, until he reached the escalator and Gate 43. He checked his watch. "Five minutes before takeoff." He ran until the shiny hall and stream of people became a blur. He ran until his crippled right leg cramped. He took the escalator three steps at a time, and when he reached the top, he dashed for Gate 43.

A few stragglers gathered about the window, watching Flight 407 await its signal from the tower to begin its taxi down the runway.

Marcus spotted his mother and Merrilee with their faces pressed to the glass that separated them from David's flight. He listened to the revving jet roar and watched David's plane begin its taxi. Helplessly, he watched Flight 407 lift into the sky as though magic, invisible hands guided the silver giant skyward, above the Pacific Ocean, where Flight 407 held its pattern until the pilot received his instructions to take his route and take away Marcus's brother, David.

In an instant the giant silver gull was . . . gone!

Clara and Merrilee watched David's plane in silence, until they felt Marcus gently caress their shoulders. They buried their faces into his chest and wept. Unconsciously, Marcus swept the straying strand of his mother's hair back into the top of her braids. He held the two women in his arms until his own silent tears began their flow down his high, flat cheekbones.

"I'll lay ya ten to one, Hanley will go to Elektra," the bartender said as he kibitzed.

Jake didn't have an inkling. It was the best-kept secret since the opening of Tut's tomb, but Jake wasn't about to let onto his buddies. He had to earn his bread. Aside from his mangled golf game at the industry's Palm Springs Open and his hackneyed Sunday tennis matches with the hottest producers in town, Jake knew how to maneuver. "Close. Close." He winked. "Getting warmer, but not hot. Not yet."

Martinellie's was doing its normal 4:00 p.m. business. Twenty-seven-year-old Jake Tohstoh, the company's hot PR man, was holding court at the bar with the regular entourage, freelancers without offices in the 6430 Sunset Building, who'd set up shop in the industry's landmark hangout.

Jake and his cronies were partial to Martinellie's Bar. It served the most sumptuous hors d'oeuvres in town, free, just a teaser before the evening's superb northern Italian fare to come. Tart veal piccata and pasta with rich sauces Al Capone would have killed for. Their tantalizing aromas still clung to the highly polished wood and brass decor, permeating the transported New York atmosphere from the night before.

Martinellie's was "The Place." No tourist would find it in his newly purchased Map to the Stars' Watering Spots that precocious ten-year-olds hawked along the Boulevard during summer vacations. Martinellie's was off the beaten track. You had to be in the industry to know about it, or at least on the fringes.

Jake Tohstoh was the moment's star. The bar buzzed with speculations about Marcus Hanley and The September Reign. It had been a month since Marcus walked out on the company with the gold mine under his arm, and it was common knowledge that dependable Jerry Goldman had been dumped after twenty-five years of service. No gold watch, just the unemployment line and a lot of crow.

Jake literally gasped when he caught a glimpse of Marcus entering the dim restaurant. He restored his cool in a fraction. "Hey-y-y, Marcus, you rascal. Some coup d'état, Babe. Some coup. Say, if I could lay my hands on a hot group like . . . what's the name of your group again?"

Marcus appraised Jake's well-worn hype. "The September Reign."

"Yeah, yeah, The September Reign." Jake emitted a high-pitched laugh. "If I could just lay my hands on a hot group like that, I'd quit the old hype game and start producing myself." He drew Marcus aside. "Whenever you're ready to start promoting their single, let me know. I mean, what the hell, I'm on the road pushing those dogs for the company. Who's to know if I slip yours into the old attaché case? Know what I mean?"

Marcus knew exactly what he meant. "I'll keep in touch," was all that he said to Jake. Right now he was looking for Jerry.

Soon the producers, songwriters, secretaries, girlfriends, hangers-on, and undercovers would be spilling into Martinellie's for the evening's cuisine and chitchat about who was in the Top Ten on the charts, who lost their bullet, and who was out. Marcus wasn't interested.

Marcus spotted Jerry in his corner booth. It was obvious that Jer was about six sheets to the wind, and Marcus couldn't blame him. So much for twenty-five years of loyalty to the company that made big bucks off his eyes and ears and then dropped him faster than you could say, "Hang in there!"

Jerry flashed an embarrassed grin when Marcus slid into the booth. He knew that he'd had too much to drink, and he didn't care. Angie still didn't know that he'd been fired. Jerry had been replaying the scene over and over in his head. How could he break the news to his wife? Angie was planning a big bash for their twentieth anniversary the following weekend, and Jerry didn't have the heart to tell her to cancel, but they couldn't afford it.

Marcus motioned to the headwaiter. "Tony, we'll both have the veal piccata. Salad, house dressing. And pasta . . . garlic and oil."

The waiter took the order and disappeared.

"I haven't told Angie," was all Jerry could say. "She doesn't know."

Marcus covered Jerry's hand with his own. "Do you think I'd

hang your carcass out for the vultures to tear apart? What kind of a friend do you take me for? You were my mentor, Jer; you helped me to make a quantum leap across the dung. You've got a job with me until you're ready to walk, my friend, and that's an order, understand?"

"I don't understand what happened. I don't understand! I don't understand," Jerry wailed. Panic welled in his throat as he watched the young black paramedic administer a shot of adrenaline deep into Marcus's chest.

Marcus didn't respond.

Methodically the black paramedic popped off the empty syringe and snapped another full load in its place. Marcus's limp body twitched.

"He's stabilizing," the paramedic announced. "We can't move him yet." He injected more medication into the IV tube attached to Marcus's pale blue vein that protruded atop his elegant hand.

Marcus felt a burning sensation for an instant as the medication traveled upward inside the vein in his right arm. He felt his body growing heavier. "An elephant must be sitting on me," he thought. He wanted to get back to the lighter feeling he had been experiencing as he floated out of his body, back into space and time. He wanted to get back to loving, to Rachel.

The instant that he spotted Rachel Allen at Jerry and Angie's twentieth anniversary party--a big success--he'd known she was special. Marcus never considered himself a romantic. He never bought into the trendy, social-gathering speculations about finding one's "soul mate," yet when he met Rachel Allen, he knew that he'd found his. He marveled at the way the candlelight played off her rich, mahogany-colored hair. He loved her deep laugh, the way she looked at him through almond-shaped eyes, as though she were suspended in another time frame, observing the world about her, yet not part of it.

Marcus and Rachel talked and talked, from the moment Jerry had introduced them. They became intoxicated by one another, giving way to the other's ideas, philosophy, loves.

Rachel magically drew Marcus into conversations about things he had never shared with anyone, and music was their mutual passion. The lanky, young genius producer coupled with the brilliant, seasoned composer. The lady had returned from her sabbatical on the mountain and found her muse. They loved and laughed. From their first meeting they were inextricably bound.

Rachel, Jerry, and Jake Tohstoh became part of the Marcus Hanley dynasty. They rode with him on the crest of his success. Marcus's publishing wing was flourishing, and he'd signed several hot new acts in addition to The September Reign, whose first three albums had soared into platinum positions on the record charts. Marcus's ingenious strategy had made the group a household name and had made Marcus extremely rich.

The industry was making snide, death-throat rattling noises that it wouldn't last, that the successful music industry scion would soon come tumbling down from his black glass Sunset Boulevard tower and splatter like Humpty Dumpty onto the streets below.

"It won't last," the bartender quipped to his usuals. "Nobody can have it all. Life just doesn't work that way. Mark my words, it's just a matter of time," he speculated while laying out the free hors d'oeuvres. The cronies at Martinelli's Bar prognosticated on Marcus Hanley's fall every afternoon at 4:00.

Work was under way on the fourth album. It was late. Everyone had gone home. Marcus was alone, working into the night. He'd sent Rachel home to put the finishing touches on the final arrangements with the promise that he'd be there shortly. He was listening to the rough vocals that The September Reign had recorded earlier in the day. He relaxed deep into his bone-colored chair and listened to the introduction. The group's signature drum roll bounced off his office walls like crackling thunder.

Marcus began to drift with the music, when suddenly the vision of the three soldiers jumped before his weary eyes and blasted their deathly, jellied flames into the room. Fear pierced his chest. He rubbed at his eyes, and the soldiers vaporized. At that very instant his telephone rang. It was Clara Hanley. Marcus could tell by the tone of her voice that she was in shock. She told him that she'd just received a telephone call from some official-sounding person in the War Department.

"It's David." She hesitated and drew in a deep breath.

Marcus could hear Merrilee's sobs in the background.

"It seems that David has been wounded." Her voice cracked in disbelief. "They told me that they're flying him home. It's bad, Marc, really bad." She broke down and began to sob.

"Hold on, Mom, I'll be there." The memory began fading. "I'm coming home."

"Take me home."

"What?"

"I want to go home." Marcus gasped against his own body fluids rising in his throat.

"Everything's gonna be all right, man," the black paramedic whispered into Marcus's right ear. He motioned the team to lift Marcus onto the ambulance gurney. "Watch out for his IV," he ordered.

The two other paramedics lifted Marcus from his bone-colored chair, now crimson-stained from his wounds. The medics dropped him onto the gurney.

Marcus let out an agonizing wail.

"Damn it," the black paramedic bellowed in rage. "Get your act together!"

Marcus was gulping for air.

"Hold on, man; hold on," the black paramedic pleaded as he plunged another syringe of adrenaline deep into Marcus's chest.

The medications burned deep into his fibrillating heart. He closed his eyes, and as the paramedics continued, a strip of film seemed to play across his "third eye," taking him back, back, back . . .

Marcus looked down at the broken figure of what had been the once beautiful David, who lay gaunt and hollowed in the overcrowded ward at the Sawtelle V.A. Hospital.

"My God," he thought, "this can't have happened to David, The Golden One." Yet it had.

The overwhelming smell of excrement, vomit and blood, masked by hospital disinfectant, permeated the ward. Marcus felt dizzy. He sat in the metal chair at the foot of the bed and gazed at his brother. He tried to avert his eyes from the tubes that were attached to every orifice in David's body, draining wounds, feeding him. Lifelines to a very long recovery. Marcus totally avoided the empty spot on the sheet that had once been David's right leg. His brother had been to hell and returned. He reached out and took David's hand in his. "Everything is going to be all right. You're home now," Marcus said.

David stared silently at the ceiling above his narrow bed.

Marcus knew that David heard him through the morphine when a silent tear ran from his hollowed right eye.

Several months of physical and psychological therapy passed

before David was moved home. He seemed to be rallying and was fitted with a prosthetic leg.

Marcus and Rachel visited often while their work continued with the group. Rachel noticed the strain on him and suggested that they take a week off to go to the mountains. He promised they would, as soon as the promotional campaign was set on The September Reign's fourth album.

The strategy had been planned for its release date to coincide with the first week in September, signaling the long Labor Day weekend that marked the official end of summer. Kids across the country would be buying the latest hot albums and tapes to get back into the swing of the new fall semester.

It would mark the next step up the mountain for Marcus and The September Reign. His timing was expertly planned.

"I always loved it here." Marcus turned and kissed Rachel's cheek as they lay stretched out on the sand in front of his mother's house. "This was my fortress away from the world," he confessed as he turned on his stomach and gazed up at the weathered house.

Clara sat on the porch with Merrilee. David was in his room.

Rachel watched Marcus's gaze, as if she could almost read what he was thinking. She scooped up a handful of warm sand and let it trickle down his spine like a rain shower.

Without looking, he reached out and took her hand. "You're the first person who's shared this spot with me."

"I'm honored to." She rested her head in the curve of his back.

He continued gazing toward the house and watched Clara tuck the familiar wisp of straying hair into her braids. Merrilee sat on the steps, and her stare told Marcus that she was a hundred miles away. An overwhelming sadness surged over him, and his entire body emitted a shudder.

Rachel turned and put a loving arm across his shoulders.

"Let's give the album another week to make sure it's on firm ground. Then it's the mountains, and Jerry can mind the store." His shudder subsided.

"No telephones," she pleaded.

"No telephones," he promised.

With that, they both turned on their backs and faced the waning warmth of the sun as it cast its sparkling light across the horizon.

A few scavenger gulls circled near the tide's edge, hunting for dropped bits of food amid the beached seaweed. Except for the sound of the gulls and the low hiss of the lapping tide, all was still. The air was clear, and you could slice the pale blue sky with a knife.

David's prosthetic leg leaned against the bed in the room that had been his since childhood. He sat solemnly in his wheelchair, stationed at his boyhood desk. He listened briefly to the gentle surf lapping outside his window and slowly gazed about the walls of his room, covered with memorabilia from his childhood, adolescence, and young manhood. Framed photos and certificates of achievement hung on the beige walls.

He smiled when his eyes steadied themselves on an enlarged snapshot of himself and Marcus, taken many summers before, on the fateful day when Marcus fell into their sandcastle and had a tantrum. "It's funny," David thought, "how painful, yet funny memories seemed so deeply etched in my brain." He stared at the photo. Both boys were flanked on either side of their long-absent father. He noticed how Marcus had tried to hide the shame of his braced leg with a beach towel.

Slowly, David glanced down at his missing right leg, blown away during a search and seizure mission in the paddies of Nam. Horrible visions reappeared before his eyes. He heard the women's and children's screams again and felt the sensation of his right leg being ripped away. All he remembered was searing pain and the smell of burning flesh.

In a trance, David opened his intricately carved rosewood treasure box that had been shipped home with him from Vietnam. He picked up his .45-caliber keepsake, snapped in a clip, and slowly lifted the pistol to his right temple.

The sharp blast reverberated across the pale blue skies. Its fatal deed jolted Marcus to his feet. Instantly, he knew David was dead.

David's funeral was a simple one. Clara wanted it that way. He was buried in the family site at Forest Lawn. Aside from the immediate family, a few close neighbors attended. Jimmy, his brother Binky, and Tim were there out of respect for the family. Of course, Jerry Goldman and his wife, along with Jake Tohstoh from Marcus Hanley Productions, attended. Marcus and Rachel comforted the stoic Clara Hanley as David's casket was slowly lowered into the ground, and the familiar lament of the lone military bugler's "Taps" echoed from the distant hillside.

Merrilee lost control when the ritual three-corner-folded American flag was handed to Clara, the final touch of military protocol for valiant service to one's country.

It was late, and Marcus was in no shape to drive. Rachel drove the white Bentley. He sobbed the entire drive home from Clara's house, and Rachel was wise enough to allow his anguish without a word.

Rachel pulled into the circular drive in front of the high-rise condominium just off Sunset Plaza. She convinced Marcus that he needn't be encased in concrete any longer, and he agreed to move into her place in the Glen when they returned from the mountains.

Richie North appeared from nowhere and rushed them before the valet had driven the Bentley into the underground parking area.

"I've finally caught up with you," he said, pushing himself between Marcus and Rachel. "You're in the map to the celebrities' homes." He panted excitedly. "My tape, man. You know, my songs. You said to put 'em on tape, remember?" he pleaded. He scrunched his forehead into a silent sob. "Remember? My songs, man. Why don'tcha give 'em a listen tonight?" He thrust his tape box at Marcus.

Marcus stared in disbelief and then turned toward the stairs.

Rachel diplomatically whispered to the persistent singer. "Please understand, not tonight," she said. "We've just come from his brother's funeral."

Sunday passed. Rachel tried to convince Marcus to stay with her and not go into the office, but he insisted. "Let me tie up the loose ends with Jerry. Then we can go to the cabin tomorrow."

"Okay," she whispered hesitantly. Anything," she thought. "Anything . . . " She watched him pull on a pair of faded denims and weekend shirt, not his usual, pristine business attire. He moved like a robot, and Rachel ached for him.

"I'll call you later." He bent down and kissed her forehead. "Give Mom a call and see how she's feeling."

Rachel smiled up at him. "I love you, Marcus Hanley."

He touched her mahogany-colored hair. "I love you, Rachel Allen."

She watched him walk out the door and winced at his slight limp.

The telephone rang and rang in Clara Hanley's house. She was too numb with grief to answer it. She sat in the corner of her living room, staring out her window toward the sea.

Rachel hung up the phone. She'd try Clara later. She glanced at the clock. It was 10:15 a.m. She knew that she was rushing Marcus, but she decided to call his office.

Marcus and Rachel were on the phone when it happened.

Richie North brushed past Jenny's desk before she could stop him. He burst into Marcus's office. Marcus glanced up from the phone the instant that Richie North drew a .25-caliber pistol. The enraged singer pointed it directly at Marcus Hanley's chest.

"You can't put me off any longer," Richie North screamed. Before anyone could stop him, he fired three shots directly into Marcus Hanley's chest.

The bullets' impact thrust Marcus hard into the back of his bone-colored chair. The receiver fell from his right hand.

Richie North stood frozen in shock.

Jenny rushed into her boss's office and went into hysterics.

Within seconds, Jerry Goldman and Jake Tohstoh were in the room. "Get the gun!" Jerry commanded. Jake grabbed Richie's arm and wrestled him to the floor. "Let it go! Let it go, before I break your damn arm!" he said, enraged.

"Call an ambulance," Jerry ordered.

Jenny ran to her desk and dialed 9-1-1.

Jerry moved to Marcus's side. "Hang in there; help is on the way," he whispered to his friend.

Rachel's plaintive voice cried from the dangling receiver.

"Jenny, talk to Rachel," Jerry ordered. He bent down and picked up Marcus's dangling receiver and placed it back in its cradle.

"It's over, Jerry," Marcus whispered. A lone tear began its descent down the slope of his chiseled right cheek.

The police and paramedics had arrived within minutes. The paramedics worked furiously over Marcus for what seemed an eternity.

Marcus was in deep shock and bleeding heavily. He fluttered in and out of consciousness during the entire resuscitation. Jerry remained by his side, watching what seemed to be brutal lifesaving techniques. He caught himself stoically and tried not to weep as he watched his friend's life ebb away.

During resuscitation the police questioned Jerry and Jake. A second team of officers questioned Jenny in the outer office while they cuffed the wailing Richie North.

Within moments after the paramedic administered the last shot of adrenaline, Marcus Hanley's heart fluttered to a final close. His erratic heartbeats fibrillated across the portable life-monitoring machine and subsided to a single dot on the screen, tripping the deadly, droning "buz-z-z-z-z."

The paramedic noted the particulars on his Arrival-Departure Sheet. "Arrival, 10:30 a.m. Victim expired, 11:00 a.m." He flipped off the monitor, and the deadening buzz stopped.

"I'm sorry. He's gone," was all that he said to Jerry as he covered Marcus's face with a blanket.

Indian summer passed, and Marcus Hanley Productions continued to flourish under the guidance of the accountants and attorneys.

Marcus had kept his word to Jerry Goldman: "You've got a job with me, until you decide to walk, my friend."

Rachel continued on for a while and then left Los Angeles

for the cabin in the mountains that she and Marcus never had the chance to share.

Fall turned into winter, and Clara Hanley remained in the weathered house. Her proud Martha Washingtons, now browned from the season, stood in their clay pots, awaiting spring to bloom again. She couldn't let go of Marcus's white Bentley. It remained parked in front of the house. Its once-gleaming, lacquered finish was dulled by the elements, and it stood as a monument to the "House on the Strand."

An early morning drizzle began, and the sound of approaching roller skaters licked into the wet pavement. Jimmy, Binky, and Tim, wrapped in rain slickers, were on their way to school. When they approached Clara's house, Binky jumped from the rear of his brother's wet, electric-blue bike and peered at the rain-soaked Bentley.

The other boys came to a reverent stop.

Binky looked up when he caught the sight of a boy pedaling by on a bike. "Hey," he called to the boy, "do you know Marcus Hanley?"

The boy shot a backward glance as he sped by. "No!" was all that he replied.

Binky watched the boy disappear down the street. "He's a famous record producer!" he yelled.

The boy didn't reply.

Binky turned to Jimmy and Tim. "I'm gonna be just like him."

"Sure ya will," Jimmy replied. He patted his little brother on the shoulder. "C'mon, you guys, we're gonna be late for school."

"I am, someday I am." Binky's voice trailed off. "Someday... someday . . . someday . . . "

If you have built castles in
the air, your work need not be
lost; there is where they should
be. Now put foundations under them.
- Henry David Thoreau (1817-1862).

My precept to all who build is
that the owner should be an ornament
to the house, and not the house to
the owner.
- Marcus Tullius Cicero (106-43 B.C.).

Lennox House

I know this is going to sound strange, but it's been haunting me for the past several years . . . Lennox House.

"Sure," you say. "Why tell me, why not tell your shrink?"

God knows. I've thought of that. I mean it is the '90s, after all. The "politically correct '90s." Good suggestion, though, but frankly, a shrink would probably want to know if I were seeing little green men talking to me from inside of my TV set. A real, burnt-out loony. And that's not the way it was.

First of all, you may know me. I've been a very respected travel writer for the past fifteen years or so. My travel guides have been published in more than twenty countries. They're great little guides for tourists and travelers, not only to the world-renowned cities, but to some quite interesting off-the-beaten-track places as well. They're quite successful little books, and I'm the editor/writer. My name is Josh Conway. Aha! The name does ring a bell. I thought it might. Well then, you can attest that I'm a really straightforward guy. I've made friends all over the world. Keep in touch with a great many . . .

"Joshua. Over here, Josh," Cassandra called from her table in the corner of the crowded café.

I pushed through the lunch crowd in the Westwood student hangout and pulled up a chair next to hers, dropping my book bag to the well-trod plank floor. She wrinkled her nose, causing her soft freckles to converge into a tiny line down its bridge.

"Hey, crinkle-nose, where's our partner in crime?"

"Jason should be here any second." She laughed. "As soon as he puts this edition to bed."

We were the devilish threesome. Our journalistic efforts converged on *The Daily Bruin* with regularity. Three devotees during our UCLA salad days, we were going to set the world on fire. It was an exciting time. So much was going on, and we loved being in the thick of things. I wanted to jump into life feet first. God, after testing our wings for four years in the School of Journalism, we were eager to get on with it. With graduation looming, we'd already set our sights on jobs with some of the top newspaper chains. Our résumés, as thin in actual experience as they were, had begun circulating out in the real world.

Jason appeared, his tangle of long red hair bounced off his shoulders as he walked toward us, and plopped down into the empty chair next to Cassandra. She impishly ran her fingers through his hair, combing it out of his eyes. "Wild man." She giggled. "Did you make your deadline?"

Jason rubbed at his tired eyes and nodded. "Made it. But I had to pare down your article, Cass; space limitations. It had to fit around the alumni ad."

"Ouch," she cried in mock disappointment. "Must art always sacrifice to money?"

How naive we were! How open and inexperienced in the ways of the world! We laughed and gobbled down our burgers and fries. *The Three Musketeers* we were . . . Jason, Cassandra, and me.

It wasn't too long after that, the three of us were making a spaghetti feed at the house Jason and I rented in Beverly Glen, a beautiful small canyon that divides the West Side from the San Fernando Valley. It seemed Cassandra was at our place more than her own dorm, and she assumed the role of our little earth mother. Graduation was two weeks off, and we felt the coming change. We couldn't be the devilish threesome forever.

We sat silently around the coffee table eating our home-cooked pasta. Finally, Cassandra broke the calm that surrounded our unspoken feelings of sadness. We sensed that soon we no longer would be in our safe and familiar academic world.

"So, Josh, are you going to shave your beard after graduation?"

I looked up, astonished. "I thought you liked my beard."

"I love your beard," she mused. "But I can't recall seeing an anchorman with a beard."

"He'll set a precedent," Jason said. "First, a world-renowned journalist for a major chain, then a seasoned broadcast journalist with a beard."

"And what about you, Miss Cassandra? Are you going to

live up to your name and four years of education? Or are you going to waste it tidying up after guys like us?" I teased.

Her pert face blushed crimson, and she slid her delicate hand along the rough-hewn table, clasping Jason's fingers in hers. "We can have it all, isn't that what they say?" she blurted out in self-defense. "Two against one; that isn't fair."

"Whoever said life was fair?" I cajoled. I scarfed up the rest of my pasta and held out my empty plate like Oliver Twist. "More, please."

Cassandra rose, diffusing my remark with her good humor, and piled more pasta onto my well-cleaned plate. She gestured around Jason's and my cramped hillside cabin. "This place could use a woman's touch."

"It's a guy place," I quipped.

She crinkled her cute nose in my face. "No, I'm not going to waste my education tidying up. You're a big boy. You can clean your own cave."

I laughed, spurting a mouthful of pasta across the table.

"Joshua, you're hopeless," she wailed.

Jason burst into laughter. "I told you he was."

She threw a dishtowel at me, motioning me to wipe up my mess. "First off. I'm going to find a job as a stringer. Then I plan to go back part-time. I want to get my MFA in literature. I want to be a novelist, eventually."

This was the first time Cass had ever verbalized what she wanted. I was impressed with her choice. "Good start. And, Jason, my long-haired friend, where will life take you?"

Jason's eyes darted toward Cass, and then he leaned back on the couch and gazed out the open window to the hillside above. "I plan on starting out with a paper, like Cass, maybe as a stringer. But what I really want to do is to produce documentaries. And down the line, start my own publishing company, a literary magazine, maybe."

Except for the sounds of the drowning traffic outside and the crickets in the hillside brush, it was silent again. The three of us threw our arms around each other's shoulders, formed a huddle, and let out a thunderous howl.

A few weeks later, we were caught in the exhilaration of graduation ceremonies. We secretly exchanged glances that would cement our pact, while a parade of speakers blurred before us and talked about our collective futures. Our classmates were a blur as well. We three knew that this was going to be it. Soon we would be leaving. In this unspoken agreement, we looked at one another. Winking. Knowing.

After the ceremonies, Jason, Cass, and I were joined by our families for a celebration dinner at Chasen's. We had become bonded, closer than blood, during our four years at UCLA. Now we were ready for the real world, or so we thought. During the evening festivities, talk abounded between our families about our wonderfully bright futures. Although I felt an underlying strain between Dad and I, as if I had somehow disappointed him. He had hoped I would follow in the tradition of the Conway men by entering the banking field. He had affected some halfhearted attempts at conversation during dinner, smiling when the three of us couldn't stop talking about how we were going to break into journalism and change humanity. How green we were!

Then life dished out the first of one of its crashing blows. A few weeks after our graduation celebration, I received a call from Mom in Connecticut. Dad was in the hospital. I had to take a fast flight back home. By the time I arrived, he was waning.

He had suffered cardiac arrest. Guilt hung over me with its heavy veil. How was I to know he wasn't well at graduation? We were so caught up with ourselves and our lives. I didn't notice his. Dad had always been a fast tracker. Banking was his life. He'd hoped I'd follow in the tradition. My younger brother was going into it. Bill was in his second year at the Harvard School of Business and was following in Dad's footsteps like his father before him. I was the rebel in the family.

Who would be there for Mom? Somehow, Dad's death cast a cloud over my choice. I remained in Connecticut for a few weeks during the first part of the summer, to help with the finalization of the family business. Making sure that Mom would be taken care of, my brother Bill would be there, and my sister Elaine and her husband, Charles, were always close by. Mom wouldn't want for anything, except for Dad. I made certain that she was okay before heading back to California, Cass, and Jason.

My heart leapt as my flight descended over the San Fernando Valley, heading toward the Burbank Airport. Although I had lived in California only during my four years at UCLA, it was my real home. It was something I can't explain. California pulled at my chest. Even though Dad was gone, and the black cloud still hovered, I felt a burst of excitement as our plane began to take its landing path. The Valley, with its patchwork quilt of green and lemon squares, rushed up at us from beneath the yellow smog blanket as we nosed down through it. It was a good touchdown. We taxied down the runway and pulled to a stop. A perfect landing.

I scrambled down the plane's metal departure stairs, bumping past other passengers, and ran toward the baggage area. "I'm home." I sighed. I rushed outside, searching the crowd for Cass and Jason, as luggage from the other arriving flights bobbed around on the carousel. Passengers grabbed up their bags, rushing off to . . .

"Josh! Joshua, over here."

There she was, my Cassandra. My freckle-faced Cass. My little pert-nosed . . . Jason was a few steps behind her, his carrot hair flying in the breeze. They tried to look happy, in spite of my loss. Smiling, waving. I knew they were glad to see me. I could feel them trying to think of the correct things to say. We hung our arms together, shoulder-to-shoulder, in our traditional football hug, as the carousel went round and round, and the other travelers' luggage continued to circle until all bags were gone.

Jason reached out and gathered my lone, battered valise with its patchwork of UCLA stickers.

"You're home," Cass said. She reached up and brushed my bronzed, bearded face with her exquisite hand. "Give me a hug."

I hugged her with all of my heart. "Oh, my God, here we are."

The sun glistened off of an infinitesimal light that shone on her left ring finger. The slightest speck of a diamond sparkled from a thin gold band that held it so proudly. "Why hadn't I noticed before, those two?" I guess I was blind. I thought we'd go on forever like the Three Musketeers.

"So, my lucky ones, when is the wedding?"

Cass blushed and nuzzled into Jason's shoulder.

"Well, buddy," Jason replied, "we were thinking of the fall. You're going to be our best man, aren't you?"

"Of course I'll be your best man. I am your best man."

We laughed. Jason paused, not knowing quite how to say it, so I said it for him.

"You can't be my roommate forever."

"I guess not, Joshua," he said.

Cass smiled, burying her head into Jason's chest.

"We want to show you something before going home. We found this jewel of a place. It's here in the flats, in the Valley," Jason said.

"We happened to run across it one day on our way to a garage sale," Cass burst in. "It was just sitting there waiting for us. We have our marker on it."

After driving from Burbank through North Hollywood, we arrived at a street called Lennox. Actually, Lennox strings through the Valley from Sherman Oaks to Van Nuys and farther on, jackknifed by side streets and the Los Angeles Riverbed.

We pulled to a stop in front of this disheveled WW II job. It looked like no one had lived there in a hundred years. A makeshift "For Rent" sign hung at an angle from the Chinese elm that stood gracefully in front of the house's ancient exterior.

"Geez, you guys have got to be kidding."

"Isn't it great?" Cass blurted in excitement. "We checked it out. It's owned by an interesting lady. Someone who'd lived here for years, but it's just been abandoned for a while. We saw the sign and fell in love with the place. We thought it has wonderful possibilities . . . this Lennox House. What do you think, Josh?"

"What do I think? I don't know what I think. I think it's going to take a lot of work. And who knows if you'll even get the place?"

"But we just feel it has our marker on it," Jason said. "You know how you get that special feeling, Josh. You just know."

I nodded. "Oh, sure. Yeah, you just know. Come on, it's abandoned."

They yanked me out of the car and led me alongside of the house. The windows were bare. Blank old eyes that held secrets. Eerie eyes. "My God, how long was this place vacant?"

"Who knows? It's waiting for us to make it our home," Jason said.

"Look in the back. I want to show you its magnificent kitchen," Cass chimed. "I can already see it brimming with friends sharing pasta."

She saw magnificence. I saw only cobwebs, piles of torn cardboard boxes, and stacks of old newspapers. God knows what else. I couldn't dissuade them. This was going to be their dream house. This was Lennox House, as Cass called it.

"It's kind of literary," she said. "I see this house, and it reminds me of Daphne du Maurier's *The House on The Strand*. Remember that novel? I always loved time-tripping stories. Can you imagine what stories these walls could tell, if they were able to talk?"

That was my first experience with Cassandra and Jason at Lennox House.

During their first three months in Lennox House, Cass and Jason had miraculously transformed the abandoned place. Gone were the cobwebs, trash, and dilapidated piles of boxes. They whitewashed the interior, and Cass created a wonderful English garden. Where there had once been only weeds, crabgrass, and rotting vines there now were bursts of color and greenery with winding rock paths. The once humble back yard magically transported you into another time frame. Borders and planters were filled with blooming impatiens, sweet Williams, rosemary, flax, and caladium and water ferns. It amazed me that she was able to achieve such wonders in the Valley's arid climate and adobe soil. It made a resplendent backdrop for their perfect Elizabethan garden wedding that took place that fall.

After the musicians, caterers, and last of the guests drifted off into the balmy evening, the three of us remained. We sat in the garden drinking champagne and listening to the sounds of Cass's handmade glass wind chimes singing in the breeze and the calming waterfall that Jason had engineered from stacked olive barrels and a small electrical water pump that he had attached to the outdoor spigot.

Finally I asked, "Why do you have two front doors?"

Cass darted a quick glance at Jason. "You saw them?"

"Yes. The first time you showed me the place. It seemed strange to me. I just never got around to asking. That was a really hectic homecoming."

"There's only one front door, Josh," Jason answered.

I shook my head. "But I got the distinct sensation of two entry doors. Am I seeing things or what?"

"No," Cass said. "At one time there were two front doors."

"When we first moved in and were cleaning up, we found a small wooden box. It contained invoices from a contractor. We were curious and read through them," Jason said.

"It seems as though the original owner had made the house into a duplex. One side was for his family, and the other was rented to another family. They had put a dry wall divider up and made two entry doors. But that was long before the lady, the current owner, bought the place. I'm amazed you picked up on it," Cass said.

I felt a ripple of a goose flesh rise on my forearms. "Next you're going to tell me Lennox House is inhabited by spirits!"

"Only benevolent ones." Cass laughed.

"Well, I find it rather intriguing. What about the lady who owns it now?"

"She's a mystery. Somewhat of a recluse, I guess," Jason said. "The real estate agent was quite secretive when we signed the lease. It seems she doesn't want us to know who she is. Just as long as our rent is on time, no questions asked."

"And what about the original owner, the one who built the separate doors?"

"The name on the invoices was a William Curry. But that was right after the war, wasn't it Jason?"

"Yeah. The dates were in 1945. Guess that must have been when the house was built," he said.

"Well, enough of this spooky stuff; this is your wedding night," I said. "And if I'm to do my duty as your best man, I think it's time you began your honeymoon. Mr. and Mrs. Jason Bronson, your carriage awaits you."

Jason and Cass sat in the rear seat of my rented Town Car as we circled the block, and I came to a stop at the curb. I opened the passenger door, extended Cass my arm, and escorted the newlyweds back to the front door of Lennox House.

Over the next several years, I was part of Lennox House. Cass and Jason became my extended family. We spent holidays together, and I watched the progress they made. None of us set the world of journalism on fire, but we found our respective niches. I ended up with a travel magazine after college, and eventually ventured into doing my own travel guides. Secretly I loved the freedom it gave me, although I never did give up the dream of someday going into broadcast journalism.

Jason worked for a local paper and taught journalism during

the evenings in the UCLA extension program. He was an excellent teacher. Cass worked on her novel. She was calling it *Lennox House*, and she spent a great amount of time working in their English garden and adding to their antique collection. We corresponded often, exchanging photos, and there was always something new to see when I visited them. They didn't have children, and I didn't pry as to the reason or reasons why. They appeared to be idyllic and happy each time we were together.

During the last several years, our reunions have been less frequent. I had been living in Europe, doing my travel guides and wandering. I guess secretly I was hoping to find my Cassandra and a Lennox House of my own. They always made me feel connected to their lives, but somehow I felt like a third wheel. "The best man," as I had joked when they announced their marriage plans way back when they picked me up at the airport after my Dad's funeral.

It had been three years since I'd been back to the States, and this time I decided not to call in advance. This time I decided to surprise Cass and Jason by just showing up on their doorstep with wine and bread and stories to tell of the wandering prodigal son.

"And, that's it. That's how it all happened."

The old couple nodded, listening politely to my story.

"Maybe you're on the wrong block of Lennox," the old man said. "Maybe the house you're describing is farther south."

"No," I said. "It's the house across the street from yours. I should know; I've been there hundreds of times. I'm not mistaken."

The old woman smiled. "We've lived in this house more than twenty years, son, and that house has been abandoned ever since I can remember. George is right; maybe the house on Lennox that you've described is farther south."

"Ma'am, the house across the street is Lennox House. Farther south is the Los Angeles Riverbed."

"Well, son, maybe you should go down to the Hall of Records and check it out. Like we said, the house across the street has been abandoned for at least twenty years."

I turned from the couple's porch and stared at Lennox House. It looked exactly as it had the first time I saw it with Jason and Cass. It couldn't be the same place. I've been there. All of their work! I turned back to the old couple, rocking in their porch swing.

"But if you've lived here all these years, don't you remember the young couple that lived across the street? There was a wedding in that house. They planted an English garden. Friends were always coming and going. I can't be losing my mind."

"I didn't say nobody was ever in the place," the old man said as he shaded his watering blue eyes with his weathered hand while staring past my shoulder into the hot afternoon sun. "The place has had a string of vagrants camping out over the years, but the police always rousted 'em out."

"You don't remember the young couple, a husband and wife? They renovated the place."

"You've had a long trip, son, and it's hot," the woman said. She poured a glass of iced tea from the pitcher that sat on the plastic yard table and offered it to me.

"Thank you, Ma'am." I rinsed it down my hot throat.

"Like George said, vagrants broke into the place lots of times. You know, hippie types, but nobody like you've described."

"What about the lady who owned the house?" I ventured in a desperate attempt to make sense of the situation.

The man scratched the top of his balding head. "If you mean Martha Gatewood? She hasn't lived there in more than twenty years."

"What happened to her?" I asked.

He shrugged his shoulders. "The story has it her husband died there, and she moved out. Abandoned the place. Never went back. She lives somewhere else, or maybe she's dead now. Never came back, if that's who you're referring to."

I handed the empty glass back to the woman.

"Like George said, your best bet is to go down to the Hall of Records and check out who owns the house. Maybe that would help you find out about your friends." She smiled.

"Thank you for your time," I replied.

They rose from the porch swing and picked up the pitcher and empty glasses.

"Happy to have been of help," the old man said. "Come on, Mother, it's time for dinner."

I watched them disappear into their house and close the screen door behind them, and then I crossed the street to Lennox House. A cold chill went up my back. "Cass and Jason, where are you?"

The windows stared, holding secrets, just like they had the first time I saw the house. Weeds and rotted vines choked the place. I walked around to the back of the house. The lush English garden and olive barrel waterfall were not to be found, as though they had never existed. I peered into the kitchen from the torn back window screen, only to see cobwebs, piles of old newspapers, and torn cardboard boxes. An overwhelming sense of grief grabbed my throat. I had to leave. I ran down the rubble driveway and got into my car. I had to find them, Cass and Jason.

As I started the car, I couldn't help taking one last look at Lennox House. I noticed its two front doors, with their antique stained-glass inserts, brightly glowing from the front of the house, and as I drove away, I swear I could hear the sound of glass wind chimes singing in the hot, silent afternoon.

One for the money.
Two for the show.
Three to get ready.
And, four to go.
- Anonymous, (British Nursery Rhyme 1800s)

Run For the Money

Richard Skylar ran. He didn't want to stop until he'd reached the point where he could no longer feel his aching legs pumping his body forward or the asphalt thuds beneath his Adidas. He wanted to run until he was free, beyond pain and memories. He ran through the streets dodging the early morning traffic. Richard listened to his own methodical breathing as the cold November air sliced into his flaring nostrils. He monitored each intake of breath as it burned into his expanding lungs and then watched it escape from his lips into bellowing puffs that dissipated as he pushed toward the grassy parkway that divided Sunset Boulevard in Beverly Hills.

Richard felt the softness of the parkway grass beneath him as he adjusted his Walkman. Bach's "Toccata and Fugue in D Minor" wafted into his ears. He bent and rubbed at his right shin as the organ's heavy dirge drowned out the commuting traffic noise.

For some who took the same route each weekday morning, he was a landmark of sorts. The lone runner, his sweat-drenched headband pulled tight across his tanned forty-year-old forehead, appeared as though a wind machine had permanently frozen his hair back from his face. He was oblivious to the stream of traffic, while listening to Bach as he cooled down. When the piece finished and the Brandenburg "Concerto No. 3 In G" began playing, he automatically pushed the rewind button on the Walkman before the tape's upbeat violin "Allegro" could continue, listening dreamily again to the organ's solemn requiem.

Rosalind had set a challenge for herself. She had committed herself to a spring showing at Gallery 150, promising its owner to come up with twenty-five new canvases that would capture the spirit of a day in the park. Many of her works already graced the walls of corporate foyers, and she thought the park would be a perfect setting for her to experiment with the new style she had chosen for the commission, to capture action events with speed and clarity using acrylics and watercolors on canvas. She set up her easel at the edge of Beverly Glen Park, confident that soon the stalwart touch football players and runners would appear that brisk November morning for their ritual workouts in the lovely little park nestled halfway up the glen from the boulevard below.

A passing commuter honked and waved to Richard from his driver's window. "Lucky stiff. Keep it up!" The commuter honked again for good measure, before turning his zombie stare back across the wheel and back to his drudging morning commute.

Richard was jolted from his reverie as the harried commuter disappeared from sight. He jabbed his toe into the wet turf while the morning blared by him, isolating him on his solitary island. The Bach fugue broke into the violin allegro before he could rewind the Walkman.

Rosalind mixed primary colors on her palette and waited for the park to fill with early morning life. She rubbed her frail hands together to take off the morning chill and then performed a series of small finger exercises as if she were a concert pianist preparing to begin a concerto.

Richard jabbed his toe again into the wet turf, and then he began running in place. Strange how time and similar weather seemed to reignite a memory. He tried to brush the accident from his mind. Soon two other runners joined him on the parkway. Three kindred souls blended as one. They slapped hands, patted each other's shoulders, and exchanged silent greetings before running off in their separate directions. Bach's "Allegro" now dissolved into his piano concerto "Italian Concerto BWV 971," and Richard didn't bother pushing the rewind button on his Sony Walkman as he darted back across Sunset Boulevard and began running up the glen.

Rosalind noticed how the morning light glistened off the treetops like diamonds. She began to fill in a yellow wash when Richard appeared from nowhere at the park edge. He startled her as he ran past her easel, stopping a few yards ahead to perform his customary cool down. She quietly observed him as she added water to the colors on her palette. He was a perfect subject and would challenge her to translate his speed and agility onto the flat canvas. Quickly she sketched his basic outline. She picked up nervousness about the lone runner; the way people behave while waiting for someone who is late.

Suddenly he stopped pawing the grass and turned toward her. His dark eyes pierced hers. "Are you drawing me?"

"Yes," she answered with a start in her voice.

"Why? I don't know you," he snapped.

Taken aback by his directness, she laid down her palette. "I'm an artist, and you're a wonderful subject," she stammered.

"You don't have my permission." He picked up the canvas and perused her rough sketch. "Not bad . . . you've captured the basic motion." He set the canvas back on its easel.

She searched for an appropriate defense. "You're right, and I have intruded on your privacy." She rummaged through her bag and came up with a card and brochure, which she handed to him. "My name is Rosalind Mitchell."

He glanced at her pamphlet. Recognition crossed his face. "So, you're the artist."

"Yes."

"You want to draw me?"

Rosalind hesitated.

"Do you?"

"Yes. Well, not exactly draw you. I'd like to paint you. Capture your essence as a runner."

"How much will you pay me?"

"Pay?" She hadn't thought about it. "You're absolutely correct," she said. "Of course you should be paid."

"How much?" he demanded.

"Well, I could offer you five dollars an hour to pose."

He looked away, disappearing into Bach's "Fugue."

"Should the piece go into a limited edition, I could pay you a royalty." Rosalind didn't want to lose him as a subject.

He turned over her business card. "Can I reach you here?"

"Yes," she stuttered.

"Good. Draw up the papers. I'll call you." He turned and began running toward the street.

"Is fifteen percent okay?" she called after him.

Without looking back, he answered, "Fine."

"What's your name?" she shouted after him.

"Skylar. Richard Skylar," he yelled. He disappeared up the glen.

Richard Skylar. The name rang a bell, but Rosalind couldn't quite place it.

"Richard, it's been nearly a year since the accident. I know how you feel, but you can't keep running away. You have to come to grips," Charles said, as he held out the year-end P&L ledger to his boss. "Clients want you, not just your associates. When will you come back?"

Richard slumped into the chair across from his chief financial officer's desk. "You're a good man, Charlie . . . always keeping me on top of the numbers." He closed his eyes, removed his sweatband, and sighed a deep, aching sigh. "I don't know if I can ever come back."

Charles set the report on his desk, absentmindedly fingering the pages. "The staff is depending on you. We're in a cash-flow crunch. Times are rough out there, Richard. Frankly, I don't know how much longer Skylar Architects & Associates can keep afloat without you. God knows the market has taken a three-hundred and sixty-degree turn. I'm just the numbers cruncher here. I don't want to be the messenger of doom, but man, you've got to make a decision."

"You know that painting I have hanging in my office?" Richard stated as he unlaced his Adidas and dropped them onto the carpet.

Charles removed his glasses and narrowed his eyes, remembering. *"The Javelin Thrower?"*

"That's the one."

"Yeah," Charles said.

"I met the artist today in the park. She wants to paint me . . .

capture the essence of the runner."

"Oh, my God, Richard. I think you should get some counseling. I'm serious, you have to make a decision soon, or the firm is headed directly for the toilet and everyone along with it."

Richard smiled a bleary-eyed smile. "I don't know, maybe I would make a good subject." He laughed.

Charles sadly shook his head.

The painting of *The Javelin Thrower* stared down from its stationary position against the white plaster wall, his poised muscles rippling beneath the painted flesh of his right arm. His javelin pointed directly toward the center of Richard's head, who eyed him from between his grungy sweat-soaked feet resting cross-ankle atop his office desk. He crossed his arms behind his sweat-soaked head and stretched back into his chair, returning the painting's stare, all the while wondering who the stranger was who had posed for the artist.

He could feel the afternoon sun warming his head from the skylight above, creating the flawless silhouette that extended skyward, forming a perfect pyramid of light and shadow within his modern enclave that he had purposely designed after the great Renaissance cathedrals of Europe.

He flipped on the Walkman and let Bach stream through his brain. Richard felt like a pile of dung, as though he were shard pieces of rock fragmenting into an old dust heap.

"What can you say, Javelin Thrower frozen on canvas? What if I don't want to come back? What if I were to freeze on the wall like you?" Richard talked to the painting hanging before him, bigger than life. "What if we could change places, you and I? I'd do it in a second if it would change things, bring them back." He choked on the tears that ran down his throat. He let his head roll to one side of his chair and looked down at the photo on his desk. Bach's piano *"Allegro Vivace"* danced inside his head.

"Pull me higher, Daddy," Jamie squealed as Richard lifted his four-year-old son by the arms and propped him on the back of his neck. His wife, Sandra, reached around his waist, hugging him just in time for a kind stranger to take their picture that day they played at Disneyland. The three of them were frozen in time.

It had been another cold, wet November morning.

"It sounded like an explosion," one of the spectators relayed to an officer who had arrived at the scene of the accident. "It all happened so fast. One second their car was traveling along in front of mine, and the next minute it went into a spin, hit the embankment, and . . . pow! Their car caught fire and crashed down the canyon. It all happened so fast."

Like the witness' account, that cold November morning Sandra was driving Jamie over Mulholland, on their way to his nursery school, their car had skidded across the wet pavement and careened down the side of the canyon, becoming their instant funeral pyre.

The Bach tape snapped off on Richard's Walkman, and he sat suspended in silence for a moment, until a dry wracking sob welled up from inside him. For the first time in almost a year, Richard finally allowed himself tears.

Slowly he pulled his aching legs down from the top of his desk and leaned his sweaty chest across it. He stared back at the painting. "It's a done deal, Javelin Thrower. We'll trade places, you and me." He reached into the pocket of his sweats and pulled out Rosalind Mitchell's crumpled business card. He gazed at it before returning it back into his pocket, and then he left his office.

Now it was Rosalind Mitchell who was the nervous one. The

name Richard Skylar finally had rung a bell, and after rummaging through her bills of sale, she remembered. Samuel, her friend and mentor at Gallery 150, had sold her painting of *The Javelin Thrower* to Skylar Architects & Associates nearly two years earlier. The signature on the bill of sale was to a Richard Skylar. It didn't make sense. If this was the same Richard Skylar she'd met in the park, why would he be interested in posing as a model for five dollars an hour?

"Maybe it's just a lark," she thought aloud as she straightened out the models' space in her storefront studio in Echo Park. "He couldn't possibly be the same Richard Skylar, the world-renowned architect and builder. It has to be a coincidence." She set up the blue-sky canvas backcloth in front of the old treadmill-running machine and brought out the large fan and spray bottles of water.

"This should simulate the park with more privacy," she convinced herself. She straightened her selection of paints, brushes, cans of turpentine, and canvas rags that crowded her small studio, setting them onto the metal shelving bolted to the sidewall of the old brick-walled converted storefront. Finally she set up her easel and palette a good distance in front of the running machine. Why did she feel so unnerved? "God, he was just another model." If he were the architect Richard Skylar who had purchased her painting for $10,000, he must have thought her work was good enough to pay such a fat sum, even though she had only received fifty percent of the asking price after Samuel and Studio 150's commission.

"It's just a coincidence," she told herself. "Same name, but not the same person. After all, such a successful architect wouldn't waste his valuable time posing as a model for five dollars an hour.

"For goodness sake, he could buy and sell me in five minutes. It's just a coincidence." She checked and rechecked the contract her friend and accountant Mark Wiseman had drawn up for this modeling session. Lord knows, she wouldn't want to cheat anyone out of a royalty, should the work go into a limited edition printing. She reread the agreement one more time. It was fair. After all, she was only an artist, not a conglomerate.

A large crashing sound sent her in an upward jolt. She turned in time to see Missy, her tabby cat, skittering along the metal shelving and knocking more cans of painting materials to the cement floor.

"Missy, you're going to give me a heart attack. Get down from there," she scolded, as Missy languidly skirted the cans of paint, turpentine, and rags sitting on the metal shelf, turning to purposely knock one or two more crashing to the cement floor below, all the while enjoying the frenzy it sent her mistress into. Rosalind frantically rushed to recover the tumbled mess.

"Missy!"

The tabby turned from her perch atop the highest shelf and began casually licking at her right, turned front paw as if to say, "Pay some attention to me."

"Mom, Mom, is that the runner? Is he here?" Arthur called out from their apartment in the rear of the studio.

Rosalind opened the door to the small living quarters that she shared with her ten-year-old son. Arthur maneuvered his wheelchair away from the Nintendo game he had been playing on his computer.

"No, Arthur, it was just Missy."

He slumped his frail body deep into his wheelchair and turned his gaze back to the computer game. "Oh. Is Missy being a little devil again?" he asked while moving his slight hands calmly along the keyboard.

"I think she is," Rosalind replied.

"Well, remember, Mom, you promised to introduce me to the runner, okay?"

"Okay."

Richard Skylar stood at the front door to Rosalind Mitchell's studio. He handed Rosalind her rumpled business card as she opened her door to let him in. "Ms. Mitchell, I'm ready to begin work."

"You're already dressed to pose," she said with a nervous laugh.

"Well, isn't that what artist's models do?"

"Yes." She crossed to her easel and began fussing with the canvas. "I've set up a simulated area of the park," she said, pointing to the blue-sky backdrop and treadmill. "I thought you would prefer the privacy."

Richard glanced around her studio, taking in every nook and cranny. "So, this is how the artist lives."

"It's where I work, away from the real world." She laughed.

"I like it. What's that smell? It smells like turpentine," he said, flaring his nostrils.

"I apologize," she said, pointing to the mischievous Missy lolling on the top shelf among the paint and rags. "Missy has been being the bad tabby cat again."

"I see," Richard said as he reached up to the top shelf and pulled the cat down against his chest. "Giving Ms. Mitchell a run for her money, are you, Missy?" Missy nuzzled into Richard's sweatshirt for an instant before bolting out of his grasp and leaping back onto the top shelf. She warily perched high above and watched the big cat people below.

Richard laughed and pulled his red sweatband across his forehead. "This is how it was in the park, wasn't it?" he questioned, pointing to the sweatband.

"Exactly," Rosalind replied. She picked up the agreement. "Would you care to go over the papers before we begin working?"

Richard shook his head "no" as he stepped onto the treadmill. "I'm sure they're fine. Is this where you want me?"

"Perfect," Rosalind stammered. "Would you care to hear some music? Most models do. It helps to get them into the mood."

Richard turned on the machine and began running in place. "Do you have any Bach?"

"I think I do." Rosalind went through her stack of CDs before picking out Bach. "Here's one."

"Do you have his *Brandenburg Concerto No. 3?*"

She glanced at the music titles on the CD cover. "Yes."

"Could we hear that?"

"Of course." She put the disc on the player, and the music filled the studio.

Richard ran on the treadmill as Bach surrounded the studio and closed in the silence between them. Rosalind turned on the fan, causing his hair to blow back away from his face as it had done naturally the day she saw him running past her easel in the park.

Quickly she began sketching him in on her white, blank canvas as Missy watched with amusement from her perch above.

Bach totally filled the studio, and the artist and model melded into one purpose.

Richard ran and Rosalind moved her charcoal and brushes

quickly across the white canvas that began to come to life, becoming more real than either of them.

As the music swelled and Richard began to feel the perspiration drench him, the memory of that cold November morning flashed inside his head. Tears began streaming down his cheeks moments before Rosalind, caught in the creation of the movement, had noticed. She caught his pain and quickly set down her palette. "Mr. Skylar, are you all right? Please, stop." She turned off the treadmill and guided him to a nearby chair. "Please, sit down. Can I call a doctor? Are you ill?" She drenched a towel with the nearby bottle of water and pressed it to his forehead. "Oh, Mr. Skylar, I'm so sorry."

Richard silently grasped Rosalind's hand and the wet Turkish towel, pressing them both to his forehead while he caught his breath. "I'm fine, Ms. Mitchell. I'm okay."

Both of them rested in silence as Bach clicked off the CD player.

Finally Rosalind broke their silence. "I don't understand, Mr. Skylar. Why you are doing this? You certainly don't need the small pittance that I can afford to pay you."

Richard let go of her hand. "Do you think this painting will be as great as your *Javelin Thrower*?"

Rosalind stepped back, shaking her head. "I don't understand."

"Do you, Ms. Mitchell?"

"Yes."

"Well, then you've answered your own question." He mopped his drenched brow with the towel and moved back to the treadmill. He straddled the machine and let his forehead rest against its cool metalworkings. Without looking at her, he drifted for a moment.

"When you gave me your business card in the park that morning, I felt a weird connection. You were the Rosalind Mitchell whose painting hung in my office, and I thought, 'This delicate woman created that strong piece of work. Amazing.'" Slowly, he turned his head in her direction. "You know, no matter where I sit or stand in my office, his eyes . . . *The Javelin Thrower's* eyes are always staring directly at me. Strange."

Rosalind smiled at Richard, feeling his pain. Mr. Skylar, you don't have to tell me if you don't want to, but sometimes we all have to run away from things for a while, to give ourselves time to heal. I believe that's why you create buildings. I know that's why I paint."

"He is frozen in time. You captured him with all of his life and focus, with every ounce of his being directed into the javelin. I thought he could literally step off the wall." Richard pulled himself upright, turned on the treadmill, and began walking slowly in place.

"We can continue the session another time, Mr. Skylar."

"Richard."

She hesitated and then repeated his name. "Richard."

"No. We'll continue today. Today is a good day. You're paying me five dollars an hour, Rosalind. Honest money for honest work."

Suddenly, a tin of brushes flew to the floor from Missy's perch above them, and the tabby jumped onto Richard's shoulder.

"Missy!" Rosalind reprimanded the cat as she rushed to rescue Richard from her cat's pounce.

He lifted the tabby off his shoulder. "She's fine." He scratched Missy behind her ear and placed her back onto the top shelf.

"Mom, what happened?" Arthur wheeled himself into the studio. His eyes brightened at the sight of the runner. "You are here. Mom said she was going to paint you."

Richard turned to Rosalind. "An accident?"

Rosalind shook her head no.

"I have spina bifida," Arthur said as a matter of fact. "I was born with it, and Dr. Rubinsky said someday I could run."

"Mr. Skylar, this is my son, Arthur."

Richard stepped off the treadmill and extended his hand in a friendly shake. "I'm happy to meet you, Arthur. Tell me, who is this Dr. Rubinsky?"

"He works with people who have spinal injuries and people born with them, like me," Arthur chimed in. "Dr. Rubinsky has invented walking systems with computers, hasn't he, Mom?"

"Yes, he has. Dr. Rubinsky believes that with the proper treatment and exercises, someday Arthur may be able to walk and run," Rosalind said. "It's in the experimental stages, and Arthur was excited to learn that a real runner was coming to pose for my painting."

"That's right. I told Mom I wanted to talk to you. She said you were a professional runner. Maybe you could give me some lessons."

Richard caught his breath. "Well, Arthur, I'm not what you would call a professional runner."

"But you run in the park, don't you?"

"Yeah."

"Then, you're a real runner. Can you show me?"

Richard nodded his head and got back up onto the treadmill. He turned to Rosalind. "Could you put on some Bach again?"

Rosalind smiled and turned up the CD player full blast.

Richard began running on the treadmill. "Now, watch my legs, Arthur."

Arthur wheeled his chair in front of the treadmill.

"Okay, Arthur, here goes. One for the money."

"Two for the show."

"Three to get ready."

"And, four to go . . . "

Richard Skylar ran as Bach's piano "Allegro Vivace" swelled with exuberance, filling the artist's studio with its glorious celebration of life.

It was your skill and science
that led you astray
and you thought to yourself,
I am, and there is none but me.
Isaiah 47:10

Just a Game

John Nance reread the biblical inscription for the third time, making certain not to let his fingers touch the center of the page. He held the letter by its outer edges. He didn't want to take a chance of ruining any prints by smudging them over with his own.

Nance remembered that bit from the security meeting Clarke held with Ronnie Everett's production staff a month earlier, soon after the first anonymous messages began arriving. As Everett's security chief, Clarke had instructed the entertainer's staff on the handling of any future messages and the nature of suspect mail procedures, particularly the accepted psychological stats on disturbed stalkers of high-profile celebrities. Clarke's seriousness was met initially with lighthearted joviality, disbelief, and denial of anything remotely sinister. Everett's staff was like one big loving family.

Nance had been with Ronnie from the old days, when he was the songwriter-guitarist member of The Crystal Troubadours, long before Ronnie Everett and Lenny Stafford had split and gone off onto individual fame and fortune as crossover country-pop stars. Even though Nance's family was quite well off, at the time they were chagrined that he chose the nomadic life of the road. They would have preferred him to eventually join his father's law practice, but Nance was an artist at heart and had been loyal to Everett since the beginning. He was now very content to work behind the scenes, coordinating Everett's career.

Patricia Williams, on the other hand, had been with them since day one, when she joined as the group's fan club president. Initially she hoped that her association with the prestigious pop group would lead to a career in television journalism. That was nearly fifteen years ago. Now she was Ronnie's personal secretary. All of the years they'd been working together, nothing like this had ever occurred. Frankly, these messages were a first for her, and she took Clarke's instructions to heart. What else could she do?

None of his staff showed it during that first meeting with Clarke and the other off-duty police officers, who made extra money moonlighting at Everett's house, but secretly they were a trifle scared. After all, Ronnie Everett had been their bread and butter for a long, long time, and that's where their loyalties rested.

Nance absentmindedly fingered the latest plain white envelope that had carried the new epigram. It looked the same as all of the others. Nothing was ominous about it. You could purchase a box load of these envelopes for pennies at any discount stationary store. As usual, there was no return address, and the postage was first class. The postmark stamp read: "Marina Del Rey." The sender could be anywhere in the greater Los Angeles area, because the Marina Del Rey postal branch processed an immense bulk of Westside mail. He retrieved the security folder from his desk and slipped the newest message inside, along with the fifteen others that bore postmarks from various parts of the country.

"Go figure," he said to Patricia Williams. "So we have some religious fanatic sending cryptic messages to Ronnie. Come on, Pat, you know how crazy his fans can get sometimes. We've seen it all."

"Let me see it," said Patricia. A tone of fear etched across her normally controlled voice.

Nance sighed, opened the folder, and held it up for her inspection.

She picked up the newest message by its outer edges, gingerly inserting it into a plastic protector, just like Clarke had instructed, and held it up to the desk light. She slipped on her reading glasses and perused the message. "There's nothing special about the paper, no watermark. It's the same cheap photocopy paper used for all of the others."

"Don't you think you're getting a bit obsessive?" Nance asked.

"We can't be too careful, John. I'll run this by Clarke and see if he can get any prints. We may just have some sort of whacko on our hands. Where did this one come from?"

"L.A., postmarked at the Marina Del Rey branch."

Patricia gasped. "Ronnie is due back next week, before the tour goes to Lake Tahoe."

"So?"

"So don't you think it's strange that the other postmarks were from different parts of the country? This one is from our own backyard."

"What do I look like, Sherlock Holmes?"

"Get serious, John, can't you see the coincidence? The

SUSAN ALCOTT JARDINE

messages seem to be following Ronnie's tour itinerary."

Nance leaned back in his chair and threw up his hands in exasperation. "Pat, you've been in this business too long. You're starting to sound like a bad script. It's just some crackpot fan trying to make Ronnie 'see the way' . . . you know, 'eat humble pie for all of your success.' So maybe he's sending Ronnie some biblical sayings, trying to tell him to meek it up. I don't know."

"Well, I'm running it by Clarke." Patricia made a photocopy of the latest arrival and handed it back to Nance. "Here's another one for your collection. By the way, has anyone told Ronnie about these?"

Nance shook his head. "Not yet. Clarke doesn't want to alarm him until he can get a handle on the sender. Besides, you know how paranoid Ronnie could get if he thought someone was stalking him."

"It's beginning to spook me," Patricia said.

Nance plodded on methodically. "Clarke figures he can trace the type of—"

Patricia cut him off. "Listen, Sherlock, do you know how many types of PCs are out there, not to mention printers and software programs? Whatever creep is sending these ditties could walk into our reception room before Clarke has had enough time to figure it out. Then what?"

"Well, you don't have to take my head off. I'm just doing my job."

"Do your job. I'm doing mine. I'm running this new one by Clarke." With that, she did an abrupt one-hundred-eighty-degree turn on her sensible shoes and slammed out of Nance's office.

"Thanks for not slamming my door," he yelled out after her. He made two fists and pressed them to his weary eyes. Maybe it was a blessing after all that Ronnie and Lenny became the superstars, not him. Who knew during The Crystal Troubadour days that one of them would end up being targeted by a disgruntled nut case? He rubbed at his thinning hair and began entering the new message onto his computer. "I'm getting too old for all of this excitement," he thought out loud.

A few days later, during their security staff meeting, Patricia read aloud a review from the *Daily Variety.* "'The re-coupling of country-pop's legendary Ronnie Everett and Lenny Stafford, their first duo performance since the breakup of The Crystal Troubadours nearly fifteen years ago, has sent concert revenues soaring. These two icons--whose solo credits need not be enumerated here--have mellowed over the years. Concert crowds have been packing venues to hear the two superstars, and they weren't disappointed. The duo received standing ovations on their solo, platinum renditions, peppered with hits from The Crystal Troubadours' repertoire. The highlight of the set—Everett and Stafford's soulful interpretation of 'Kindred Heart,' penned by former member Johnny Nance, brought the audience to its feet. Nance's bittersweet lyrics were a standout during their 'remember when' medley. But sorely missing from this triumphant Redoux was Nance with his affable puppy-like grin and sweet acoustic riffs. Their current tour has captured new audiences for both Everett and Stafford and has definitely recaptured nostalgia boomers, like this reviewer, who remember them when. Kudos notwithstanding, next time, guys, persuade Johnny Nance to join in. 'Johnny, we remember ye when.' The sold-out Everett & Stafford: Redoux Fifteen-City Tour ends this weekend at Lake Tahoe. A definite must see, should you be so lucky to scalp a ticket.'"

She finished reading and set the trades on the gleaming marble conference table. All eyes redirected to Nance who was visibly embarrassed by the reviewer's accolades.

"Great review," Nance said, looking down at his hands.

"Terrific," said Patricia. "Now, what do we do about Tahoe? Ronnie's due back this afternoon from Nashville."

"I talked to Lenny this morning, and he plans on meeting this afternoon to go over details about the show. I think they should be told," Nance suggested.

Clarke opened his file, exposing the plastic protected messages. "It's been taken care of. Perkins has already alerted the authorities in Tahoe on the possibility of a stalker. Extra security is already in place."

"What about the type of computer, anything there?" Nance asked.

Clarke read from his notes. "We've traced it to a possible laptop; that's all we've been able to come up with. As far as the fingerprints, in addition to both of yours, there were distinct prints on all of the messages, but we haven't been able to come up with a match. We've run them by the authorities in all of the cities that appeared on the postmarks, which coincided with the Redoux Tour itinerary—"

"You see, I was right," Patricia interjected.

"But whoever they belong to either doesn't reside in any of the locales or has no previous criminal record. We've come up to a dead end, but we sent a copy of the prints and messages to the Tahoe authorities to run through their computers. We'll just have to play it by ear until we hear," Clarke added.

"I still vote that we warn Ronnie," Nance insisted.

"I plan on doing just that," Clarke said with professional

aplomb. "Oh, by the way, there is definitely one thing we do know from the prints."

"What?" chimed Nance and Patricia.

"They definitely belong to a male. I'll be going along with Perkins to pick Ronnie up at LAX. I'll brief him on the way back from the airport. We can prepare Lenny at the meeting."

After Clarke left the conference room, Patricia shot a suspicious look toward John Nance.

"What?"

"Nothing."

"Pat, what are you thinking? I didn't do it."

"I didn't say you did."

"Right. Well, Clarke said both of our prints were on the messages, along with the nut who sent them."

"Let's see if Clarke comes up with anything between now and the meeting," Patricia suggested.

"Yeah," Nance said with resignation in his voice.

Lenny Stafford arrived a bit early for the meeting and was happy to find Nance alone in his office. "Johnny, me lad," he quipped and gave him a bear hug.

Nance jumped about ten feet from his chair.

"Didn't mean to scare ya, John."

"It's okay, I've been a little preoccupied. Hey, congratulations on the tour. The reviews have been great."

Lenny dropped his canvas bag on the floor and plopped into the guest chair next to Nance's desk. "Johnny, you've got to come with us to Tahoe. The reviews were right. You're sorely missed. Come on, John, just one more time. It's the last show." He grinned like a burly teddy bear.

Nance smiled at his old friend. "Always the cheerleader, Lenny.

No, you guys are the stars now. Besides, I'm rusty as hell. I'd just screw up the set."

"Don't give me the old humble-pie routine, John. Ronnie and I've discussed it. What else do we have to do between shows?" He winked. "We would love to have you there with us. Until this tour, we had no idea that everyone loved the old songs so much." He patted Nance on the back. "Do it for The Crystal Troubadours."

Nance laughed. "Let me think about it."

"Good. While you're thinking about it, I need you to do a favor."

"Sure."

Lenny retrieved his canvas bag. "It's my laptop. Somehow, I must've screwed up. I can't get it to print."

"Let me take a look at it." Nance opened the computer case, turned it on, and pulled up a file.

It was your skill and science
that led you astray
and you thought to yourself,
I am, and there is none but me.
—Isaiah 47:10"
popped up on the screen.

"Where did you get this?"

"I picked it up at a discount store—"

"The message. Where did you get it?" Nance demanded.

"Hold on, John," Ronnie said.

Clarke and Patricia were hedging behind him.

"You don't understand what's been happening here," Nance said.

"I understand. Clarke explained everything."

"I just asked John to check out my laptop. It's jammed."

"They have been receiving your messages," said Ronnie.

"My backup?"

"Right, but we forgot to tell them."

"What?" Lenny was doubly confused.

"About the game."

"'Breaking the code?"

"Yeah. Why don't you let them in on it?"

"We should have told you, but we wanted to work out the bugs. You know, how much time you have on your hands during a tour. So Ronnie came up with an idea to develop an interactive game. That's why I was mailing the epigrams back to the office. I'm not a whiz like you, Johnny, so I mailed the epigrams as backups. I was right. Somehow, I screwed up my laptop."

Nance and Patricia looked relieved.

"Oh, sure," Nance said. "A computer game. Why didn't we think of it?"

Clarke felt a little sheepish. "If everybody will excuse me, I'll call authorities in Tahoe." He made a hasty exit.

"Thanks, you guys, for being so concerned," Ronnie said. He turned to Nance. "Will you join us in Tahoe, for old times' sake?"

Nance shook his head and grinned. "I'm rusty as hell, but why not?"

"Good, we'll discuss it over dinner at the house."

Patricia lagged behind. "I'll follow you. I'm just going to lock up."

"Okay." Ronnie winked, and then he wrapped his arms around Nance and Lenny. "Lighten up, John. It's just a game."

After everyone had gone, Patricia went about methodically straightening up the offices, neatly stacking papers and magazines, putting everyone's phones on the answering service. She took one final look, picked up her purse, and turned out the lights. Just as she was about to lock up, she was greeted by a mail carrier.

The young woman handed her the special delivery. Patricia signed for the letter, retrieved her reading glasses, and opened the envelope.

The gamester, if he dies a martyr to his profession,
is doubly ruined; he adds his soul
to every other loss, and
by the act of suicide
renounces earth to forfeit heaven.
—Colton

Patricia's hands trembled as she turned over the plain white envelope. The postmark read "Lake Tahoe." She ran back into the office and dialed the phone. "Clarke . . . Clarke," she screamed. "It's not just a game."

There is no such thing as chance;
and what seems to us the merest
accident springs from the deepest
source of destiny.
- Johann Christopher Friedrich von Schiller,
(1759 - 1805)

The Channel

"I will not take no for an answer," said Roberta Rosner with a slight edge of bitchiness in her voice. "It's been over a year since Daniel dropped out of your life, with not so much as a Christmas card. You can't squirrel yourself away in your apartment forever, Ellen. Life is waiting for you to rejoin it."

Ellen rolled her eyes ceiling-ward while awaiting the cashier to tally up her lunch tab.

"I can't believe you're still mooning over him, after he dumped you for that out-of-work starlet when he handled her divorce, and he's not even a divorce attorney."

"You needn't announce it to the world," Ellen snapped.

"After all," Roberta went on, "don't you think you would have heard something from him by now if he gave a damn about you?"

Ellen paid her tab with embarrassment, as she noticed the young male cashier's interest in her coworker and best friend's advice. The cashier nodded and then added, "She's got a point there, lady."

Ellen scurried through the crowded Hilton cafeteria toward an available table, Roberta pacing briskly behind. She scrunched into an empty chair, hoping no one else overheard her friend's well-meaning comments. Brushing her hand through her cap of Orphan Annie curls, she stabbed silently at her veggie plate in hopes that Roberta would lay it to rest. She thought of the times she had called Daniel and, getting only his answering machine, didn't have the courage to leave a message. She'd hoped maybe she would receive at least a call or a word of reconciliation, a Christmas card, Valentine's Day card, an Easter card, a Bar Mitzvah card . . . anything that showed he cared. Nothing. Just messages from relatives, telemarketers, requests for charitable and political donations, and wrong numbers. Daniel always said he was not one for sending cards. Nothing in writing. "Nothing incriminating," Ellen thought. "Always the lawyer."

But the forthright Roberta Rosner had not laid it to rest. She set her tray on the table with a confident sweep and, without missing a beat, doused her herring salad with a fresh wedge of lemon before continuing. "Am I right, or am I right? It's time to get out into the game again, meet some interesting people. After all, Ellen, how many relationship books can you read?" She cherished her first bite of herring salad as if it were the most tantalizing thing in the world.

Ellen felt the stab of truth. Her fork dropped to her plate. Mustering courage, she shook her sandy curls nervously. "That's a cheap shot, Roberta. Besides, what makes you think I'll meet someone at a séance at the New Vision Bookshop . . . except, maybe a dead person?"

Ellen's offhand remark made Roberta laugh. She couldn't cover the deep chortle that slipped out of her lips. Hah, there still was some fire left in her friend. Life's unrequited love blows hadn't dampened Ellen's spirit yet. Roberta eyed Ellen with affection and then patted her hand. "Alexander is one of the, if not the, most renowned channels in today's metaphysical world. The most interesting New Age people will be there. Ellen, this is not an event that Los Angeles experiences every day."

Ellen dabbed at her untouched veggie plate. "When is it?"

Savoring the pause and relishing her last morsel of herring salad, Roberta placed her utensils on her clean plate before answering, a definite twinkle in her brown, almond eyes. "Three weeks from Saturday. Eight P.M."

"Let me think about it," was all that Ellen said.

On their invigorating walk back to the Beverly Hills office complex where Ellen and Roberta worked, a fleeting thought crossed Ellen's mind. "What could she lose by going to hear the channel at the New Vision Bookshop?"

Something strange was definitely happening to Ellen. She found that she was beginning to misplace things, her glasses, car keys, an appointment book. She even stopped herself one morning as she realized she was putting the clean silverware into the refrigerator. One afternoon, after reading intently, she placed the novel into the refrigerator as she pulled out a carton of milk to mix herself her afternoon energy drink. It drove her crazy for the better part of the day. She was in the midst of the most dramatic part of the plot and was dying to know what happened between Bruce and Gilda, but she was damned if she could find her romance novel.

She began to take notice of the series of little mishaps and memory lapses that seemed to be occurring more and more frequently. A definite pattern was beginning to emerge. Thirty-three-year-old Ellen Hancock couldn't be going through a mid-life crisis, or could she? "No. Just put that thought out of your mind, Ellen. That's not the case." But something was definitely off kilter.

Roberta Rosner's words echoed in her head. "Alexander is the most renowned channel in today's metaphysical circles."

"Ellen, you're being an absolute paranoid. Don't be so uptight, just because Daniel called Jeffrey. They're both on a nodding basis, colleagues. Maybe they're working on a mutual contract—same project, separate clients, so what's the big deal?" Roberta's muted voice questioned on the other end of the line.

"All right, all right . . . don't push, Roberta. You know how I like to think things out, plan my life. So I'm not as impetuous as you." She dropped her receiver into the cradle.

The three weeks until D-Day had swept by, making Ellen an inconsolable wreck on the Friday afternoon before the awaited Alexander event, and now, the call from Daniel had made it worse. Her high-tech phone burped, and Roberta's extension flashed once again across its digital display.

"Jeffrey would have mentioned it to me," Ellen ventured, a quiver in her voice. Her eyes darted suspiciously toward Jeffrey White's office door, adjacent to her secretarial bay at the prestigious entertainment law firm. "I'm his right arm. He tells me everything. When I answered and heard Daniel on the other end of line, I coughed and disguised my voice, so maybe he would think I was a temp. God, Roberta, Daniel knows where I work. How could he be so cruel as to call here for business? How could he?"

Roberta softened her normally assertive tone. "Ellen, you know as well as I do that personal feelings are exempt from the deal game, particularly in this town. Detach, honey."

"Well, when he shows for the meeting, I'm going to be sick. Jeffrey will just have to call for a temp. What does Daniel expect me to do, lie down on the rug and play dead?" She caught her breath before continuing. "Thanks, Roberta, I'll see you at the New Vision Bookshop. Tomorrow at eight P.M." Ellen watched extension 232 evaporate from her digital telephone display.

She stared again at the tiny screen that flashed 5:00 P.M. "Why can't I be more like Roberta?" she thought. "Why can't I detach?"

The balmy summer evening was a perfect time for Ellen to discard her widow's weeds. Throngs of weekenders were strolling along the renovated Third Street Promenade, eating in the quaint sidewalk cafes, enjoying the street musicians, and enjoined in groups of intellectual discourse. A Renaissance of the marketplace and cultural establishment had been consummated in those few short blocks on the West Side. As she neared the New Vision Bookshop, her brand-new pumps tapping quickly against the promenade's tile pathway. Ellen gasped. Massive crowds of New Age people were already packing into line. She looked down at her attire. She was totally out of place, overdressed. The New Agers were casually dressed. Jeans, T-shirts, Hip Hop rappers, cutoffs, even Indian saris. Ellen realized she had overdone it in an attempt to fit into "the game" again, as Roberta had called it. She felt her black linen suit and patent pumps would have been more apropos for a funeral. It was too late. She was there. What could she do? She spotted Roberta swathed in a gold, silk sari. A lapis lazuli swung from a gold chain that encircled her long Egyptian neck, set off by her overpowering mahogany hair. "My God, she's Nefertiti reincarnated."

"You can look at the sale tables on our way out," Roberta said.

Ellen dropped the rose crystal she had been admiring back into its velvet display box, as she allowed Roberta to rush her up a crowded aisle toward the stairwell at the rear of the bookshop. "Where are we going?" she asked, her eyes widening to catch a glimpse of all the New Agers mingling, chatting, and browsing.

People were already crowding into seats in the upstairs salon. Stage lights were directed toward the small elevated speaker platform. A young man with a very Steven Segal ponytail was adjusting a microphone in front of a high-back Elizabethan-looking chair. Another technician was adjusting the gels on the lights, bathing the chair in soft pink.

"Here," Roberta whispered. "Let's sit up front."

"But all the chairs are taken," Ellen said.

"On the floor," Roberta said. In front of Ellen's eyes, the reincarnated Nefertiti slid to the floor like a prima ballerina doing Swan Lake. Roberta became the flawless supplicant awaiting the master, as the pink light backlit her mahogany hair to perfection and her golden sari draped around her.

Ellen, trying to be inconspicuous, crouched down on the floor. Her tight black linen skirt and patent pumps made it impossible for her to do it gracefully, more like a dying duck than Roberta's exquisite swan. She caught a glimpse of a cameraman from a local cable station. "Oh, my God, I hope they don't show this on the news," she thought. "Daniel always tapes this station's ten o'clock news."

Roberta stared toward the Elizabethan chair, transfixed.

Ellen removed her shoes and scrunched down, trying to look as though she weren't there.

The salon lights began to dim and the New Age din dropped into a magical silence. The hush was broken by Paul Winter's "Morning Echoes" wafting over the speaker system. As a key light illuminated the speaker platform, a woman in a floral dress stepped up to the microphone. The music lowered and underscored her welcoming speech.

"What's with the hat?" Ellen whispered, eyeing the woman's gold lamé hat that reminded her of an inverted lampshade, the way it sat stoically upon her curly, brown head.

"Shhh," Roberta whispered.

"Ladies and gentlemen, it gives me the utmost pleasure to introduce the renowned Mr. Bo Richman," the woman said, adjusting the microphone as it reverberated "RICHA . . . MAN, RICHA . . . MAN, RICHA . . . MAN," until it echoed to a normal tone. "Mr. Bo Richman."

Ellen elbowed Roberta. "Where's Alexander?"

"Just listen," Roberta murmured.

Ellen's shoulders drooped as she stared silently at the Elizabethan chair, ever the dutiful child.

Bo Richman appeared in the key light, nodding a thank you to the lady in the lampshade hat as she made a swift departure to a seat near the platform.

"Ladies and gentlemen, I am delighted to be here tonight for this prestigious event. Alexander has much information to impart to you from the other side. The new millennium is rapidly approaching."

Ellen eyed Bo Richman with curiosity. She watched a small-framed man dressed in a blue plaid sport shirt and tan khaki pants take his place in the Elizabethan chair, which seemed to overwhelm him. "This couldn't be him," she thought. "He looks like Herbert, my accountant."

He brushed his tousled grey hair away from his gold-rimmed glasses and smiled a beatific smile before continuing his address to the New Agers. "For those of you who are new to Alexander, let me give you a brief history," he said in a mellifluous voice. His gaze seemed to be directed at Ellen.

Ellen attempted to scrunch down lower, but her knees were already aching from digging into the carpet.

"Before Alexander made himself known to me five years ago, I was a normal, simple accountant," Bo Richman continued.

"I knew it," Ellen mumbled under her breath.

Roberta shot her the evil eye.

"My life was quiet, a simple life. Aside from my accounting practice, I enjoyed working in my rose garden, reading, attending occasional lectures and concerts, nothing spectacular. I knew nothing of trance channeling or metaphysics. My work and life, for that matter, was very linear. Windows and doors on the balance sheet, as they say." He chuckled and tossed his grey mane out of his eyes once more, sinking deeper into the velvet Elizabethan chair.

Ellen stared. "What's the gimmick?" she thought.

"Then one evening, five years ago, as I was walking home from my office, I crossed the street, and wham . . . I was struck by a hit-and-run driver. After three weeks in a coma, I awakened in the hospital and found I was able to channel, although I didn't know what channeling was."

Ellen gasped and leaned forward, mesmerized.

"Can you imagine how bewildering this was?" said Bo Richman. "I thought I was losing my mind. I found that if I walked past someone, I knew what he was thinking. I would take on other's feelings as though they were mine." He paused and smiled at Roberta. "I thought I must be beyond schizophrenia. I seemed to have hundreds of personalities, and there was nothing on which to hook them."

Roberta returned his smile. Ellen eyed their exchange.

"Then one evening I was explaining this phenomenon to a group of friends. They were intrigued and baffled. It was so unlike me. Suddenly I stood up and started speaking to each of them . . . telling them things about their lives that I had no way of knowing, giving them messages from someone called Alexander. After that happened, I sat down and had no recollection of what was said. My friends told me that the messages were true, accurate." Bo Richman drew in a deep breath and clapped his ethereal hands together with enthusiasm.

Ellen felt a chill run down her spine as her recent memory lapses flashed across her mind.

"That evening totally changed my life," Bo Richman said. "There was a young woman present in the group, a friend of a friend, who explained to me what was happening." He nodded to Roberta.

Ellen gave Roberta a "you never told me about that" look.

"And from that point on," he said, "my spiritual work and study began with the being from the astral plane who will speak to you this evening . . . Alexander."

Ellen, completely absorbed, watched as Bo Richman put himself into a trance, and before her very eyes, the modest accountant seemed to transform himself into a past age presence of incredible power. His entire body changed in front of her. His soft voice became strong and resonant. The entity of Alexander began to speak in a Gallic and jocular tongue through the passive vocal cords of Bo Richman. His own voice lost its precise meter and became lost in a thick, old Irish accent. He bent forward, his eyes wide open, yet he was not of this world.

"G'd eve, m'darlin's. M'ladies 'nd m'gents. M'lads 'nd m'lassies. 'Tis me, Alexander . . . here w' ye again. Ahh, what a spritely group w' ha' here t'nite. How fortunate t' be here amongst ye." Bo Richman--Alexander--thrust his right palm toward the ceiling, as if to push off some unseen thing. "A'right, a'right," he said. "There'r so many spirit guides tryin' t' come forward this eve . . . they 're so excited, so many things t' tell ye."

Ellen's eyes darted about the room, looking to see . . . what? She turned her attention back to Alexander.

"Well, many a challenge 'r upon ye . . . ye earth people livin' in the new millennium. Many challenges loomin' b'fore ye. Well, then, each century has i's own challenges, doesn't i'? 'N now, thee twenty-first century is upon ye. Ye are livin' in the most marvelous o' times. For the visions o' the prophets 're upon ye," Alexander said. He relaxed back into the soft velvet of the Elizabethan chair, taking in a deep breath before continuing.

Ellen looked about her, seeing the audience of New Agers rapt with attention, knowing something that she didn't. "My life has been a paperback romance," she thought. "I've been hidden somewhere in a box. Where have I been?"

Alexander leaned forward, exuberant. "Ye souls livin' on the earth plane a' this time will experience the great conjunction o' y'r solar system . . . Uranus 'n Neptune. A planetary event th' occurs every one hundred 'n seventy-one years, resultin' i' the chaos 'n upheaval ye ha' been experiencin'. Many souls ha' incarnated t' be on the earth plane t' guide others t' the higher spiritual light durin' such tumultuous times. F'r out o' the fire comes the spirit risin' t' higher levels o' understandin'."

The pain in Ellen's knees evaporated as she listened to the information Alexander imparted. She had completely lost sense of herself, no longer self-conscious, just conscious. Alexander's lecture seemed to take minutes. After he finished passing on information from himself and the other spiritual guides, he narrowed his attention to individuals in the audience, those with personal questions, which he answered. After a brief silence, he turned his attention toward Ellen.

Ellen's self-consciousness returned. She stared down at her hands, folded on her lap, hoping that Alexander would avert his eyes to someone else. He didn't.

"Young w'man, d' ye ha' a question f'r Alexander?"

Ellen slowly raised her eyes. She felt hot. Perspiration beaded across her nose as she realized that the cameraman from the local cable station was focusing on her face. "No," she answered.

"Oh," Alexander said. "Why d' I think ye d'?"

"I don't know."

"Ye don't know?"

"No, not really."

"Why does it show i' y'r aura? A name is comin' t' me . . . i' starts w' 'n E. . . Esco. Escobar. Does tha' mean somethin'?"

"Yes," Ellen replied.

"Ye ha' come through a sad time, a time o' loss o' a love. Ye ha' been i' mournin'."

"How does he know that?" Ellen thought, hoping somehow Daniel's VCR had miraculously broken. "Yes, I guess I have," she confessed.

"Alexander knows ye ha'. Tell us, what is y'r profession?"

Ellen squirmed. "Just a secretary," she said, embarrassed

that she didn't have a fancy title like manager or director. "Just a secretary." She watched as Alexander's lungs seemed to puff up like bellows, ready to add fuel to the flame.

"Just a secretary!" his powerful Gallic tongue exploded.

Ellen cringed, waiting for the final embarrassment.

Alexander's tone softened with great love and caring. "Ethereal Sunburst," he said.

Ellen looked at him in disbelief.

"Yeah, Ethereal Sunburst. 'Tis the name ye guides ha' giv'n ye. They ha' been tryin' t' ge' through t' ye, make contact'. Tha' is why ye been experiencin' strange things, lapses i' yr' memory. But ye 'r a stubborn spirit." He laughed warmly.

Ellen gave Roberta an astonished look. Roberta smiled and nodded.

Alexander continued. "How could ye b' ashamed o' such a holy callin'? Don't ye know where the word 'cleric' comes fro'?"

Ellen shook her head.

"Fro' the clergy. The clerics, the scribes 'n the priests. The keepers o' the Holy Word fro' the beginning o' humankind. Ye ha' chosen a holy profession, Ethereal Sunburst. Secret...ary," he said. "Keeper o' the Holy Writ . . . the secret word passed down fro' the priests, clerics 'n scribes . . . the mystery o' God himself. 'Tis a blessed callin', a sacred callin'."

Tears welled in Ellen's eyes.

"'Tis time f'r ye to discard y'r widows' weeds, Ethereal Sunburst. They were yours fro' many lifetimes past. 'Tis time f'r the younger souls t' carry o' the manure. Tha's why the guides ha' been watchin' o'er ye, preparin' ye to continue y'r chosen work 'i this New Age. 'Tis time f'r ye t' dance i' the merriment o' the flowers tha' come forth fro' y'r pain. Ye ha' much work t' do . . .

o' a joyful nature." Bo Richman--Alexander--smiled at Ellen. "D' ye know tha' God seems t' choose cracked vessels t' carry forth his work?"

With that, Ellen watched Alexander miraculously fade away as Bo Richman came back into his body. He pushed his grey hair away from his forehead and smiled at the audience of New Agers who began to push toward the speaker platform, and then he stepped down and greeted Roberta.

"What a blessing to see you in the front row," he said, as he hugged his friend.

Roberta turned toward Ellen. "Bo, I'd like you to meet a dear friend of mine, Ellen Hancock."

He reached out both hands, clasping Ellen's outstretched hand in his, with not a semblance of recognition of the dialogue that had passed between them. "What a pleasure," he said.

Ellen smiled and nodded.

The lady with the lampshade hat appeared at Bo's right elbow, a slight tinge of jealousy in her voice. "It's time for us to go, now," she said, smiling at Roberta and Ellen. "The cable station wants an interview." She began to pull him toward backstage.

Bo turned back. "I'll call you, Roberta." He smiled at Ellen. "On your way out, stop at the crystal table. They have a lovely collection of rose quartz crystals that you might like."

"I will," Ellen replied.

Roberta grabbed Ellen's hand and led her downstairs in the direction of the crystal table. "You see?" She smiled. "There are some things I didn't tell you. You don't know everything about me."

"I'm so glad," said Ellen, squeezing her friend's hand. "Thank you for a wonderful surprise."

When Ellen arrived home, she kicked off her patent pumps and dropped her black linen suit to the living room floor. Feeling totally energized, she headed straight for her refrigerator. As she opened it, she let out a little gasp when she discovered *Bruce and Gilda* wedged under her carton of milk. "Oh, there you are," she said as she pulled the paperback romance out of the refrigerator, and then she remembered what Alexander had said.

"Tha' is why ye ha' been experiencin' strange things, lapses i' y'r memory."

Thinking of Daniel Escobar, she dropped *Bruce and Gilda* into the trash. "Life isn't a paperback romance." For a moment, Ellen thought she could hear Alexander's warm laughter echoing in.

"I saw you on last Saturday's ten o' clock news," Daniel Escobar said as he passed his right forefinger across Ellen's rose quartz crystal that rested on her desk.

"Really?" said Ellen, looking him straight in the eye.

"Um huh." Daniel noticed the stack of metaphysical books next to the rose crystal. "You've changed your reading habits. No more paperback romances?"

"Yes. No more paperback romances," said Ellen.

Daniel's manicured fingers adjusted his silk Bijan tie as he smiled down at her. "Did the channel . . . what was his name?" Daniel asked.

"Alexander," Ellen replied. Realizing her mourning had ended, she felt released.

"Yes, Alexander. Did he say anything about me afterwards?" Daniel asked, curiosity in his voice.

"No," Ellen said with a smile. "He looks like he's just stepped out of a bandbox," she thought, to paraphrase her grandmother.

Daniel was still as handsome and confident as ever, meticulously dressed. The shock of silver hair brushed back from his widow's peak, looking as though it were intentional, sweeping through his jet-black hair. She remembered how she had teased him, saying he must have colored it. His silver streak had been a private joke between them.

"Oh," he said, disappointed. "Well, maybe we could do lunch soon."

"Maybe."

Jeffrey White's office door opened, and Jeffrey stepped out to greet Daniel Escobar.

"Well," he said, extending his hand to Daniel, "I see you and Ellen have already met."

"Yes. You have good taste in secretaries," Daniel said with diplomacy.

"Thank you. Particularly since you will be joining the firm," Jeffrey announced, "it's well that you and Ellen become acquainted."

Daniel stepped back and then covered his insecurity. "I didn't think the firm was to make an announcement until the papers were signed," he ventured.

"Not to worry. We haven't," Jeffrey confirmed. "But there are no secrets between Ellen and me. She's my right arm."

Daniel, relieved, smiled at Ellen. "Of course."

"Anything you need to know about clients or cases, just ask Ellen," Jeffrey added.

"I will," Daniel replied.

As Jeffrey White ushered Daniel Escobar toward his office, Daniel glanced back toward Ellen for an instant. In a patronizing tone, he commented, "It seems odd you would choose such a

Holly Golightly as your right arm."

"What a blessing," Jeffrey whispered. "She seems to have come out from the black cloud she'd been under for the past year. Most likely an ill-fated romance. I didn't pry."

"Oh?" said Daniel Escobar as the door closed behind them.

Ellen ran her right forefinger across the rose crystal before her telephone burped its ring. Extension 232 flashed across its screen. "Hello, Roberta. No. I'm fine. I didn't throw up on the rug, call for a temp, or play dead."

Roberta laughed on the other end of the line. "Good. I'm proud of you." She paused. "There's someone here who stopped by to visit me and wants to talk to you."

"Who?"

"Hello, Ellen. This is Bo Richman," the soft voice said from Roberta's extension.

"Oh, hello, Mr. Richman," Ellen said.

"Hello. Roberta suggested I speak with you. It's regarding a book . . . about Alexander."

The old fear rose in Ellen's chest. "Jeffrey didn't tell me anything about a book."

"Who's Jeffrey?" Bo Richman asked.

"My boss."

"Well, this has nothing to do with your boss," Bo Richman said, clearing his throat. "You see, we've published pamphlets and newsletters only about Alexander so far. Now there is quite an interest in this phenomenon, and I'm finally ready to start thinking about a book . . . about the information that Alexander channels through me. Roberta thought you could be of assistance, in an editorial sense. Would you be interested?"

Ellen was silent.

"Are you there, Miss Hancock?"

"Yes."

"Well, may I take you to lunch so we can discuss it further?"

"Yes, I think I could do that."

"Do you know a good place?"

"The Hilton cafeteria is just a few blocks away. We could chat during our walk there."

"That sounds wonderful." Bo Richman chuckled.

Ellen envisioned him brushing his grey locks away from his gold-rimmed spectacles. "What are you wearing?" she asked impetuously.

"A blue plaid shirt and khaki trousers." He laughed. "What are you wearing?"

"A white linen tunic and tie-dye skirt."

"I thought so," he replied.

For an instant, as extension 232 faded from her digital display, Ellen swore she felt wings on her heels.

About the Author

Born and raised in Los Angeles, Susan Alcott Jardine majored in theatre arts at El Camino College and California State University Los Angeles. She worked briefly as an actress in theater, television, and film before working behind the scenes in music production/publishing as a writer/editor for entertainer Kenny Rogers' *Special Friends* newsletter, in entertainment law and broadcast television. While studying screenplay, teleplay, and playwriting in the Writers Guild USA West, Inc.'s Open Door Writing Program, Susan and her writing partner Marc Havoc received The Writers Guild Foundation Award for their screenplay *Lullabyeland*. Susan is also a painter, and her artwork is in private collections in the US, San Salvador, and Kenya, East Africa, including the permanent collection of Providence Saint Joseph Medical Center. She lives in the Los Angeles area with her husband, Neal; their many rescued cats; and a contingent of interloping critters.

To contact the author, please send correspondence to:
Susan Alcott Jardine
Green Door Editions
P.O. Box 56839
Sherman Oaks, CA 91413-1839
Email: susanajardine@GreenDoorEditions.com

For a schedule of author events and news about *The Channel: Stories from L.A.*, please visit:

www.GreenDoorEditions.com and
www.outskirtspress.com/SusanAlcott Jardine

Book clubs and reading groups, to order books in wholesale quantities of 10 or more, contact:

Outskirts Press, Inc.
10940 S. Parker Road - 515
Parker, CO 80134
1.888.OP.BOOKS
1.888.208.8601 - Fax
www.outskirtspress.com
www.outskirtspress.com/BuyBooks

LaVergne, TN USA
26 October 2009

161937LV00002B/4/P